A

Robert Houghton

story

Also by this author:

Smoke and Mirrors
— the first Robert Houghton story

———————

The Tin Box
— a treasure hunt for younger readers

Engines of Change

Marian Bond

The right of Marian Bond to be identified as the author of this work has been asserted by her in accordance with the Copyright, Designs and Patents Act, 1988.

ISBN: 9798577010379

Independently published

With thanks to

Charlie, Jim and Kath

14th September 1824

The mail coach *Silver Mercury* bumped and rattled along the 'turnpike' en-route to London. Three of the four inside-passengers had joined the coach at the start of its journey in Birmingham. After initial polite introductions and inconsequential conversation, they had withdrawn into their own thoughts and had spent most of the journey in almost complete silence. The fourth passenger was a smartly-dressed man in his early thirties who had recently boarded at Edgware. The new man, Edward, smiled and looked his fellow passengers over. He took particular notice of another young man who had the look of a resigned but apprehensive traveller. Edward noted he was well-dressed but not ostentatious and he looked unused to coach travel as he spent much of the time looking out of the window rather than passing the time with a book. Edward said nothing.

The fellow-traveller was Robert. Originally from Westmorland he had spent most of his adolescent life working at his brother's cotton mill in Manchester. Following a terrible tragedy at the mill Robert had become estranged from his brother and was starting a new life in London as an engineer. Unlike his first coach journey from Kendal to Manchester eleven years before, when he shivered and shook on the outside seat of a lumbering stage-coach, he could now afford the luxury of an inside seat and the faster travel of a Royal Mail coach. Instead of clutching a humble bundle of clothes, his possessions were safely stored in a deal box in the boot of the carriage.

The journey was a long one. It had already taken Robert a day to travel from Manchester to Birmingham, where he had stayed overnight in a coaching-inn. The inn, although a regular stopping place for travellers, didn't seem to welcome outsiders and provided, Robert thought, very poor accommodation. The only food available was a thin stew which contained very little meat (although a good helping of gristle) and a few lumps of unidentifiable vegetable. The room, which he had to share with another traveller, had barely enough space for the bed and an old worm-eaten chest of drawers. He was thankful the sheets were clean but still woke in the night bitten in several places by bedbugs or fleas. He was glad to rise early and leave again at six a.m.

This second leg of Robert's journey would take another eleven hours. So far, his fellow-travellers had bothered little with conversation, giving Robert plenty of time to consider the wisdom (or otherwise) of his London adventure. He was, therefore, pleased when they were joined by a gentleman, a little older than himself but with a welcoming smile and nod as he climbed into the carriage. They fell into easy conversation.

"Good afternoon, Robert started, "Are you joining us to go to London?"

"Aye, I'll be glad to arrive, that's for certain."

"It's been a hot and dusty day today, but I suppose that's better than riding through thick mud. I've come from Manchester and two days on the road is enough for anyone. I'm Robert by the way."

"Edward, Eddie to my friends. Aye, this is a journey I've made many times and I'm always pleased when it's over."

Robert explained that he had recently been involved in installing steam-powered stationary engines at his brother's mill and now he was going to use his skills and knowledge at an engineering works in London. Eddie listened with interest, asked questions and made concurring comments.

An older man in the carriage looked up and gave Robert an almost imperceptible shake of his head. Robert half-noticed but dismissed the old man as being irritated by the exuberance of youth.

It transpired that Eddie was originally from Yorkshire but now was working in London, also as an engineer. "I'm working with Mr Brunel. I don't expect you've heard of him but he's done a lot of work for the Admiralty. He's working on an idea for a tunnel under the Thames."

"*Under the Thames*! Is that possible?"

"Well, *he* thinks so, and so do his backers, I suppose. His son has just joined us too. He's about your age," Eddie said, looking Robert up and down. "He's got a good head and an eye for detail. He'll probably make a fine engineer one day."

******

Eventually, in the late afternoon, the coach passed through Kilburn tollgate, its approach announced by the post-horn and their journey unimpeded. Robert knew the spires and chimneys of London would soon be in view. The coach continued apace down the route of the old Roman road and then suddenly swiftly turned left. The coach lurched to one side and all the passengers fell sideways on top of each other. Robert was afraid they would overturn.

"I've ridden with this driver before," Eddie explained. "He's come this way ever since these Saint John's Wood villas have been occupied. He says it is to avoid the congestion of the carriages and carts along Oxford Street but I think he is hoping that when the householders require a coach, the *Silver Mercury* will be the first they call to mind!"

Instead of rows of terraced houses, as Robert had expected, they passed through an area of fine individual villas with their own grounds.

"It is a very modern development," Eddie continued, "The architect has made great play of his innovation. That was Lord's Cricket Ground, we just passed on our left. Do you play cricket?"

"Oh no," Robert replied. He had read about cricket but had never played or even seen a cricket match. He didn't want to make it known that for most of the people he was acquainted with, there was little time or opportunity to be involved in such an unproductive pastime. "Cricket seems to be all about making wagers on the result rather than enjoying the sport."

The coach turned another corner and passed over a busy canal. Quickly changing the subject, Robert commented, "There seems to have been a lot of new building around here."

"Ah, that is the Regent's Park. And these are Nash's new terraces. He plans to build villas too. It is the rage at present."

The last few miles of the journey passed pleasantly as Eddie showed off his knowledge of the myriad of London streets and sights. He guessed Robert would have little knowledge of city life. Robert had to admit that although Manchester was a growing town, bustling with trade and commerce, it still was a long way from the size of London.

Finally, they arrived at the inn at Snow Hill. The coachman deftly turned the coach off the road and through the narrow arch to the yard and stables. The passengers climbed off and out of the coach and waited for their boxes to be unloaded.

Eddie's was out of the boot first and the men shook hands as Eddie made ready to leave.

"Do you have lodgings for tonight?" he asked.

"Er, no, I assumed I would stay here tonight and then make more permanent plans later."

"I have a better proposal, if you will allow. I stay at the Axe. It is only a short way but our boxes are heavy. We can hire a hackney coach and travel there together. I'm sure they will find room for you."

Unsure if his new acquaintance had an ulterior motive such as robbery or worse, Robert hesitated. "Come," Eddie insisted, "We can dine together and pass a pleasant evening playing cards before returning to our labours tomorrow."

Robert still hesitated, the inn here looked as good as any and he hated cards. Then he thought Eddie had seemed genuine enough during the journey and a friend in this huge city would be a comfort. "Very well," he said. "Where do we get a coach?"

2

14th September 1824 (evening)

As the two men alighted from the hackney coach Eddie dug into his pocket. "Ah, I have no coin to pay the driver. Can you lend me the fare?"

Robert emptied his purse into his hand and held out the money in his open palm. He had a several pennies, ha'pennies and some silver. Eddie deftly plucked out two shillings and walked over to the driver. He then seemed to stand and talk with him for an irregularly long time. It seemed a lot of money for the very short journey they had just made but Robert knew London would be different to the ways of Manchester and he guessed more expensive too. Robert wondered how Eddie would have paid if he had not been there to 'lend' him the money.

They lifted their boxes and carried them inside.

"Ev'ning Silas," Eddie greeted the landlord. "My friend here is seeking a room for the night, maybe longer. Can you accommodate him?"

The landlord took his pipe from his lips and

scratched his temple with the stem. "Backroom, on second floor's empty. 'E can 'ave that."

"What are the terms?" Robert enquired, anxious not be stung for a second time that night.

"Fourpence a night, 'cluding 'n ev'ning meal. Monies in advance."

"That sounds agreeable. I'll pay you for two nights."

"I'll show you the way," Eddie offered.

They lugged their boxes up the rickety stairs. Eddie dropped his off in his room on the first floor before they continued to the floor above. The room at the back overlooked a small courtyard and several other buildings. If he cricked his neck and looked at a certain angle Robert could see a little patch of sky. Other than that, the only view was walls.

The room itself was small but surprisingly neat. No carpet on the floor but the boards were swept and there was no pungent smell as there had been at the Birmingham inn. A chest at the foot of the bed was empty of belongings, and insects. He pulled the covers of the bed back with some trepidation and was relieved not see anything scurry for cover. With growing confidence he smelled the pillow. Well-used but not repugnant.

He hoped he would not be staying at the Axe for long so decided not to unpack. He also felt his belongings would be safer kept securely locked in his box. He'd been warned about thieves and divers and felt a need for a heightened employment of vigilance.

Robert returned to the bar-room. Eddie was already there, seated at a table with a tankard of ale and a plate of steaming food in front of him. "Jenny, fetch the same for my friend here." Eddie gestured for Robert to join him at the table. Robert sat, still a little wary. Despite his misgivings, Eddie was a personable character and seemed knowledgeable about engineering. Time slipped by easily and no playing-cards were produced. Eventually, after more ale than he was used to, Robert retired to bed. He had an early start in the morning.

******

By seven the next morning Robert was seated in a hackney coach for a second time, this time on his way to the premises of J Cooper Esq.

The current Mr Cooper – John – was the third generation 'J Cooper Esq.'; his grandfather, Jeremiah Cooper had grown rich building coaches. Indeed, the style of coach called the *Cooper Flyer* was still a common sight on turnpikes all over the country. His son, Joshua Cooper, also had an astute eye for business and had seen the canals as an opportunity. He set up, first a forge and then a foundry, making everything from the picks and shovels to build the canals, to the great iron hinges for lock gates, to the very barges themselves. He had left a thriving enterprise to *his* son who continued both with the lucrative canal work and also, on another site making bespoke carriages for the very wealthy. He lived in a new and fashionable terrace in Chatham Place in Hackney but his foundry was a mile or so distant, to the east and downwind, close by Hackney Marshes.

Robert's hackney coach drove first through the busy narrow winding streets of the city, past terrible run-down terraces that reminded him of the worst places in Manchester. Then the traffic lessened and the density of buildings reduced. They passed more new dwellings but these were much more unassuming than the ones he had seen yesterday. Eventually, it seemed, they had gone beyond the edge of the city; he could see fields and cows and the odd collection of buildings.

They stopped beside a large wall and tall wooden fence surrounding a brick-built building. The journey had lasted the best part of an hour and Robert was anxious how much the fare would be. Six shillings! Perhaps the high price of the fare on the previous evening was not so unreasonable. Robert carefully counted out the exact fare and handed it to the driver. Having caught the tone of Robert's northern accent, he tetchily whipped his horses into action and, mumbling something about "Foreigners", quickly turned the carriage back to the city.

A double gate, large enough to let carts in and out, led into a smallish yard with more shed-like buildings. The thud of a huge hammer and the smell of hot metal pervaded the air. It all seemed very small and claustrophobic compared to the size of the plot of land on which his brother's cotton-mill business stood. Was there really anything to be gained by working here? Had he left a thriving industry and walked into something with no future?

The interview with John Cooper went well; Cooper was impressed with Robert's knowledge and, when he was shown around the works, with his skill on a lathe. Back in the office Mr Cooper confided that although stationary steam engines had a promising future as modern 'workhorses' in mines, for pumps and for lifting, the plans were to develop an engine that could be fitted to a carriage and take passengers in more comfort and safety than by the current horse-drawn coaches. Robert sat silent for a moment. In two days he had heard of two wild schemes that, although attempted before had never been successfully achieved. London was indeed an amazing city, full of pioneering engineers – or crazy dreamers!

"Do you think you are up to it?" Robert was roused out of his thoughts by Mr Cooper's question.

"Yes. Yes sir," he replied. Not entirely sure to what he had agreed. His full attention was now on the gentleman behind the desk. "You'll be working with our chief engineer. We have to keep ahead if we are to be leaders in this field." He went on to lay out the terms of Robert's employment. Eighty pounds a year and starting tomorrow. It all sounded very satisfactory to Robert.

As Robert left the works his first notion was to find a hackney back to his lodgings, but the thought of paying out a huge fare yet again made him change his mind. It was a fine September afternoon and filled with high spirits from his success and thoughts of his future, he decided to explore the area a little and to walk the five or so miles back to the Axe. The walk gave Robert time to think. He could not continue to travel so far to work each day. The fares alone would eat into his income and the wasted time was a great inconvenience. Perhaps he would be able to find lodgings nearer the works. As he walked south and west in the hope he was heading towards the great metropolis, he passed by one of the newly constructed terraces of houses. They were modest but reputable-looking, and then, as if in answer to an unsaid prayer, there was a house with "ROOM TO LET" on a notice in the window. He knocked on the green wooden front-door, hoping someone would be at home.

"Good afternoon," he greeted the young woman who answered the door. A small child joined her and peeped shyly from behind her skirts. "I see you have a room to rent. I wonder if I could see it."

"My 'usband's not 'ere at present. Can y' call back later?"

"Oh dear," he replied a little crest-fallen. "I don't live near here and it will be difficult to come back. When are you expecting him?"

Not sure whether to give a stranger this information, she hesitated. "'E won't be long. 'E's usually back by sunset."

Robert looked at his pocket watch and considered whether or not to delay his journey back. "All right," he smiled. "I'll call back later." He reckoned it was about an hour until sunset. He wasn't sure how he would occupy that hour but at least, he thought, it would give him time to weigh up the neighbourhood.

He walked eastwards for a while. He passed fields of cabbages and recently-cut grain and smelt the cow-sheds long before he saw them. Occasionally, by the roadside there would be a pile of stones, ready for filling the inevitable holes and ruts that the rain and frost of winter would cause. As he walked further he could see a crowd of people advancing towards him. At first he wondered who they could be and why so many were heading in the opposite direction to himself. As they got closer he could see they were mainly women, young and old, chatting as they walked, oblivious to the stranger negotiating his way past them. Soon his curiosity was quenched – the women were leaving their place of work at a mill after the day shift. He passed the works and was surprised to see such a thriving business so far out from the centre of the city. He continued walking and then took a road that headed south west. Now there were fewer buildings and even a small wooded area. In passing, he noticed some of the fields were just bare muddy patches, not because they were freshly ploughed but compacted and barren, no use for crops or pasture. He reckoned the farmers of London must be very poor at their job to let the land deteriorate to such a state and caught himself thinking about the rolling green fells back at his childhood home in Westmorland.

Some of the fields had deep pits dug in them and crude sheds erected nearby. Robert guessed the farmers must be trying to rectify poor drainage on their land and remembered his Dutch friend and colleague back at the Manchester cotton mill – he'd bc able to sort them out.

Realising he didn't actually know how to get back to the house for his appointment he considered retracing his steps but then the road turned north again and he soon found himself amongst a familiar cluster of buildings. Sporadically a carriage or horse and cart would go by, travelling into or away from the city. He passed a number of people walking along the dusty road but even if they looked at him, they didn't speak. Housing was becoming established in this outlying area of London but he felt Hackney must be a lonely place to live if no-one had the inclination to pass the time of day. Not for the first time, he wondered whether his moving to London had been wise.

3

15th September 1824

The evening had turned chilly and the euphoria of his success in the afternoon had worn off. With some trepidation Robert knocked on the green door again. This time the master of the house was at home. He was a little older than Robert, not tall but wiry and the setting sun emphasised the flecks of red in his hair. He momentarily weighed Robert up before shaking his hand and welcoming him into his home. They stepped from the street into the living room. Robert could hear his wife busy in the scullery but she did not join them. Robert introduced himself and explained his reason for wanting to rent the room. The man, who introduced himself as Spencer Taylor, seemed satisfied that he was genuine and could pay the rent. Robert looked about the room as they spoke. The couple were obviously not wealthy but the house, this room at least, although simply furnished, was kept clean and tidy.

Spencer took Robert up the narrow wooden stairs that led off from the corner of the living room.

Robert's room was at the back, the bedroom at the front being for Spencer and his wife and child. Robert guessed they needed the extra income to help pay their own rent. The back room wasn't large but was tidy and there was no smell of damp. The only furniture was a rough chest of drawers and a bedstead.

"We'll give you sheets and a blanket, of course," Spencer said, noticing the bare mattress. "The terms is one-and-six a week, with an extra two shillin's if you wants a dinner and yer laundry done."

Robert did a quick calculation in his head – yes, he could afford that, no problem. The two men shook hands and returned downstairs. Spencer led them to the scullery and introduced his wife, Lizzie. Then he showed Robert the little patch of land at the back of the house. He was obviously very proud of his 'garden', though to Robert it was a sorry scrap of mud and clinker. Linen hung forlornly on a wire washing line, a clump of Michaelmas daisies brightened the otherwise glum space, and in a corner, a few straggly tomato plants clung on to life. Now in the shade, they presumably saw sunshine during the daytime hours as he could tell there had been fruit on the plants. A few small tomatoes were still gaining what nourishment they could from the yellowing stalks as summer gave way to autumn. Spencer picked a couple and rubbed the skins beneath his fingers. "Try one," he said as he offered a tomato to Robert. Robert reluctantly bit into the tiny fruit. The skin was tough but the juice was surprisingly sweet.

"And here's the privy!" Spencer announced proudly. "It's an earth closet and the waste is put to good use."

Robert reconsidered the tomato he'd just eaten, but didn't pursue the topic.

******

With terms agreed, Robert left the Taylors, promising to return the next day. The light was failing quickly now and it was still a long walk back to the Axe. He was wary of every passing stranger and dark corner. "Don't be silly," he said to himself, "London's no worse than Manchester for robbing and murder." He didn't find this thought at all reassuring and walked with an urgent pace and beating heart to get back to the Axe as quickly as he could.

Silas was at his usual post when Robert entered the inn. He looked up to acknowledge the incomer and with a perfunctory "Ev'nin" returned to his reading. As Robert mounted the gloomy stairs, he idly wondered what preoccupied Silas's attention. A newspaper? He doubted it given their cost and the unlikelihood of Silas ever having had a political thought. Robert wagered *he'd* never attended a radical meeting or a rally, as Robert had on numerous occasions in his younger days in Manchester. The memory of Peterloo made him shudder and the reflection that so little had been achieved made him angry and despondent in equal measure.

Even as he entered his room, Robert felt something was amiss. He glanced around and lit a candle from the meagre fire the maid had lit in the grate. There wasn't much 'room' to peruse and then he noticed it – the lock on his box was awry and broken. He opened the lid and found what he dreaded. A leather purse full of money had gone. The thief had left his papers and other important possessions but had taken the readily identifiable bag of money. Grateful for small mercies and thankful he'd taken some of his wealth with him, Robert hurtled back down the stairs.

"I've been robbed!" he exclaimed.

Silas looked up, unperturbed. "Robbed y' say? Do yer 'ave proof?"

"Well, yes, my purse of money has gone."

"Did anyone see y' with a purse of money?"

"No. I was careful to conceal it." Seeing which way this conversation was going, Robert realised Silas was going to say if he couldn't prove he had a purse of money, he certainly couldn't prove it had been stolen. "It must have been someone in the inn," Robert continued.

"No one gets in or out of that door without my seeing them. Are y' saying it was **me** that stole yer money?!" Silas's temper was rising in a most uncomfortable fashion.

"No, no, of course not," Robert stammered. "It must be someone staying or working here."

"I can vouch for all my staff and all my guests. **You** are the only stranger 'ere!"

The truth was beginning to dawn. "Where's Eddie?"

"Eddie the Fly? 'E's off on one of 'is trips again. Won't be back for a day or so."

"Eddie the Fly." Robert pondered. "Why do you call him that?"

"'E's like a fly on the wall. Picks up all kinds of useful intelligence. Good memory too. Can 'old a conversation with anyone, from a Lord to a servant girl – makes them all feel special." Silas leered in a way that made Robert's insides squirm.

"And does he often bring unexpected guests to rent a room?"

"Quite often." Silas's grin was more than unsettling.

"And do they all complain of being robbed?"

"Some do, some don't." His manner continued unruffled.

"What a fool I am," Robert thought to himself. "Eddie is no engineer. Just a clever trickster. Let me think he was making conversation but all the time he was letting me do the talking. I bet that stuff about the tunnel under the Thames is all flimflam too. I've got no proof and Silas isn't going to do anything about it. Probably in on the fetch. And that hackney driver. They did seem much too friendly."

More glad than ever that he had found lodgings in Hackney, Robert sat in the bar-room in silence, still fuming at his naivety. Jenny brought him his evening meal, with a shy smile and a reluctance to look him in the eye. Even the meal was an insult – more gristle than meat and swimming in fat. It made the Birmingham fare seem like a feast! Tomorrow he would cut his losses and start afresh.

"This is the young man I was telling you about." John Cooper introduced Robert to Walter, their chief engineer. The men shook hands and Walter enquired about Robert's background with steam engines. Robert explained how he had been part of a team that had set up a steam-powered loom in the cotton mill in Manchester, and all the subsidiary work they had enabled the steam engine to do. He thought it wise not to mention the dreadful disaster that had befallen the mill – after all that had nothing to do with the steam engine itself. Luckily Walter did not pursue the subject; it was Robert's technical skills he was interested in.

Walter led Robert down from the office and across the yard to a long, rectangular brick building. It had windows high above the ground just under the roof-line – high enough that no-one could see in but large enough to let light into the structure. A chimney at the far end belched smoke and the large doors in front of them were wide enough to allow carts to enter two-abreast. They entered through a small door set in these larger doors.

At one end of the shed some men were working at a furnace and hammering hot metal, others were busy filing and honing bits of machinery. But Robert barely noticed them; his attention was grabbed by the creation in the centre of the floor. It was a carriage, or at least a cart, for it had four large cart wheels set beneath a chassis. Nothing was built on the chassis, so no place for goods or passengers, and where the shafts for the horses should have been was nothing but an iron shaft bearing two more, smaller wheels. At the back, though, tall iron pipes rose into the air, surmounting a confusion of more metal pipes and boxes laid on and under the chassis.

"This is the *Journeyman*," Walter announced proudly. "At least it will be when it is completed." Walter explained how the *Journeyman* was going to change carriage travel and transportation of goods in the future. "You see the furnace here," he pointed to a large box-like structure, "will heat the water in the boiler. The fumes are expelled through these flues and steam from the boiler will drive this shaft which in turn will propel these large wheels at the back."

Robert took a moment to take it all in.

"How do you steer it?"

"These two wheels at the front will be attached to a *tiller* that the coachman can move from side to side and so turn the carriage."

"And what about the smoke and the risk of explosion?"

"Well, there is no smoke, or none to speak of. The fuel will be coke or charcoal and anyway the swift movement of the carriage will carry the smoke, such as it is, away behind it." Far from being annoyed at Robert's questioning, Walter was pleased to be able to allay the fears that others had raised when the contraption had been first mooted. "As for explosion, there is no worry. The spherical construction of the boiler is as sound as can be and as the whole vehicle will be built of iron and steel there is no danger of a fire."

Robert walked around the vehicle, his eyes following the convoluted arrangement of pipes and shafts, slowly building up his understanding of the great invention. "And what is my task?"

Walter took Robert to one side, as if he didn't want the other men to hear his conversation. "We are experimenting with ways to make the engine more efficient. We know the vehicle will run on the roads, indeed we have had trials out towards the marshes. But when it is completed there will be the additional weight of the carriage itself, and of the passengers or freight. Our denigrators will say, 'What is the use of a conveyance that purports to have the power of ten horses when it can only run as fast as a dog cart!?' We are looking for new eyes and a bright brain to help us overcome this, er, small difficulty."

Robert prickled with excitement. There was a challenge indeed. Could he really be at the forefront of modern engineering? Mr Cooper must have thought so, or he would not have employed him. "Can I see the plans for the machine?"

"Yes, of course, they are waiting for you in the office."

******

Robert had spent the day studying the plans and discussing the exact construction of the *Journeyman*. It was lot to take in. Although the principle of adapting a stationary steam engine that propelled belts and shafts to one that propelled itself was simple enough, the new technology required innovation to overcome new difficulties. His head swam with questions and ideas as he walked back to his new lodgings. He had dropped his box of belongings at the house on his way to work that morning. The box had been too heavy to carry all the way from the centre of the city and so, once again he had been required to hire the services of a hackney driver. It struck him that the new transport would not be popular with those fellows!

Lizzie Taylor greeted him a little shyly and left him to unpack and arrange his belongings in his room. "Supper'll be ready shortly," she said as she escaped back into the safety of the scullery.

Unpacked, Robert was unsure what to do next. Mrs Taylor was painfully shy and awkward when her husband was not at home. He didn't want to unsettle her but felt he could not sit aimlessly in his room. He took a book that he had just put in one of the drawers and ventured downstairs. There was no door into the scullery, just a curtain across the doorway. He knocked on the door jamb.

"Could I trouble you for a glass of water?" Lizzie took a cup from a shelf and poured the water from a jug on the table. "Take a seat in the parlour," she said in her best English, as she handed the water to him, anxious not to appear inferior to their new lodger but feeling totally overwhelmed.

"Thank you. Ah, hello. What's your name?" Robert spoke to their young daughter who was busy playing with a doll fashioned from a ragged piece of cloth. The child looked up. "Primrose," she replied, checking with her mother that it was all right to talk to the man who had just come into the house. Lizzie smiled. Primrose waved the doll at Robert. "Is this your dolly?." he said in reply.

"Don't you be bothering Mr Houghton, now," she scolded gently but relaxing a little.

"It's no bother," Robert continued. "She puts me in mind of my youngest sister – although she would consider herself all grown-up now!" He laughed but inwardly was transported back to those happy days on the fells when Rosie was just a baby waddling in the yard and chasing the hens. It seemed a lifetime ago.

The front door opened. Spencer had returned from his work. Lizzie was at ease now and started to spoon a vegetable stew into dishes.

As they ate their simple supper together Primrose played contentedly on the floor, stacking pots, one inside another, taking them out and re-stacking them in a different spot a few inches away. After supper Lizzie took Primrose up and settled her in her bed. Robert helped Spencer clear away and wash the dishes.

"Our little bit of sunshine," Spencer said, nodding upstairs towards Primrose. "She lights up our life; deserves a name that does the same." His face changed, "She 'ad a little sister too, but we lost 'er a few mumfs back. Just free mumfs old, she was. Took by the measles."

Robert was about to commiserate but Spencer continued, "Lizzie got it too. She was proper poorly. Thought I was goin' to lose 'er too, I did. But she pulled frough, eventual like. We was lucky little Primmy was at 'er granmuvver's when it took 'old. Kept 'er there 'til it was all over. She looked for Esther when she came back of course, but after a while she stopped asking for 'er and we guess she 'as forgotten about 'er now.

Poor Lizzie's 'ad a rotten time. First 'er parents goes within six months of each other, then Esther, then I lost m' job…. Still things is lookin' up now." He grinned, willing himself to believe 'their lot' really was improving.

A team of men loaded the *Journeyman* onto a low cart and, pulled by four strong horses, drove the heavy vehicle out to the lonely roads close by Hackney Marshes. It was dark and raining, no moon, and eerily silent apart from the rain and the rumble and crunch as the unwieldy train made its way to the trial grounds. It was Robert's first experience of one of these night-time excursions and he was filled with excitement and expectation.

They had tried day-time tests in the past but the vehicle had caused such consternation from the passing public that they had taken to night-time testing only. In fact, some had been so frightened by the machine that letters had appeared in the press calling on the banning of all such experiments in public places by such 'wild and dangerous fire balls'.

The latest development on the *Journeyman* had been to the cylinders. By improving the accuracy of boring out the centres, the pistons that moved inside them glided with ease and without loss and waste of the precious steam.

In pouring rain, with water running off their cumbersome oilskin coats, the men carefully manoeuvred the machine onto the road, lit the furnace and waited for the gauges to show she was 'up to steam'. With a 'pilot' precariously balanced on the beam and holding the tiller, and the 'fireman' stoking the furnace, two men pulled away the chocks from beneath the drive wheels and the 'engineer' lowered the lever to allow the first measure of steam to pass into the cylinder. The engine hissed as the condensing chambers came into action and slowly, very slowly, the *Journeyman* began to move. It was two hours since they had left Cooper's yard and so far they had moved two feet.

However, the test went well. The new pistons were showing their worth. They reckoned *Journeyman* had achieved five miles per hour for the first time. After a night's work and buoyed by success, the men, horses and machine made their way back to the yard. The rain had eased and daylight was just breaking. Robert could see a mist rising from the dykes and ditches on the marsh and cows grazing on the rich pasture. Keeping the waters of the marsh under control by careful draining and channelling allowed the otherwise boggy land to be tamed and used. He noticed the farmers and custodians of the marsh were using faggots of wood, or fascicles, to secure the banks here and there and remembered the navvies who had built the canal near his brother's cotton mill had used the same method to reinforce the banks there. Then a thought struck him.

******

A group of workmen cleaned and prepared *Journeyman* after its outing, rather like a team of grooms caring for a prize stallion. Other men stabled and fed the horses and the chief engineer and his assistant sat in an office discussing the night's work.

"We're still lacking power," confessed Walter as he studied the plans for a thousandth's time.

"The pistons did their job though," Robert added enthusiastically. "But the boiler is inefficient. It takes so long to get to steam. The faggots made me think."

Walter looked up, puzzled.

"You know," Robert continued, "The bundles of wood along the banks of the cuts. Much more efficient than a single tree trunk. We can use that!"

"Go on," said Walter, still unsure of Robert's meaning.

"In the boiler. We spend time and energy heating a large body of water from a single source of heat. Suppose we made the boiler with lots of tubes inside, each carrying heat from the furnace. We'd heat the water more quickly."

Walter nodded thoughtfully, "Yes, that might work!"

Soon they were drawing and redrawing plans with Robert's suggested alterations.

The skilful metalworkers in the foundry built the boiler with the new arrangement of pipes and valves, and weeks passed as they modified and improved the design. Eventually a prototype was ready for testing. The change had given the *Journeyman* a certain stylishness, Robert thought. The boiler and furnace were now more closely connected and meant the body shape was a little more compact. The slope of the pipes inside the boiler made the outer casing look elegant and modern.

Once again the skeleton chassis and engine were loaded onto the cart and trundled towards the marshes. It was a cold, clear, frosty night. The wheels crunched through icy puddles. The grass and vegetation alongside the road sparkled in the light from the lanterns. The breath from the men and horses condensed into little clouds. The sky shone with a million stars. Robert looked up, mesmerised by the enormity of the sky and how the same stars had shone out for eternity; how men in ancient times would have seen the same patterns of lights. He wondered what the men who had just invented the wheel would make of their experiments.

Robert and Walter climbed onto *Journeyman*'s chassis, along with the three men who were to drive her. The fireman signalled that she was up to steam. The engineer pulled the lever and the carriage rumbled forward. Wrapped in a heavy woollen greatcoat and wearing thick leather gloves to protect his hands from the ice-cold iron tiller, the pilot pulled his hat closer on his head in readiness for the run. Walter and Robert held their pocket watches in preparation to measure the time that the vehicle would take over the eight hundred and eighty yards used to measure its top speed. With the fireman stoking the furnace as swiftly as he could, *Journeyman* gained speed and jolted and lurched over the road surface. Walter and Robert grinned to each other as they held on to the framework of the vehicle, in fear of being thrown by its boisterous passage along the road. At last they passed the flag indicating the end of the test and the engineer slowly brought *Journeyman* to a halt. Exhilarated and smut-covered, Robert and Walter checked their measurements.

The new design and subsequent amendments to the engine were a success! The time to fire up was significantly reduced and the efficiency of the steam significantly increased. *Journeyman* had reached the literally breath-taking speed of ten miles per hour.

December 1824

It was still dark as Robert made his way home; the sun would not rise for another two hours or so. Even so, the roads were quiet for that hour of the day. He went into the house as quietly as he could, undressed and climbed into the little bed. He pulled the covers closely around him. Even the cold of the sheets did not trouble him for long. He soon fell into a deep, contented sleep.

He was woken a few hours later by the sound of the family coming in the house, and Primrose's excited chatter. Through the blur of his dreams he suddenly remembered: it was Christmas day! The family had been to the morning service at the nearby church and now they were preparing to walk the mile or so to Bethnal Green to spend the day with Spencer's sister and mother.

"Christmas is a time for fam'lies," Spencer had insisted a week or so ago. "You can't get to see yours so you'll spend it with ours!" The sentiment was kind and generous but just now Robert would have been happy to stay just where he was.

Soon they were on the road, heading south. Lizzie was carrying a bundle with some small pies she had made, and Spencer had an armful of leeks – all to add to the celebration feast. Primrose trotted along, holding her father's free hand. The men chatted as they walked.

Robert learned that Spencer now worked at a nursery not far from Robert's own place of work. "Always been veg'able growers round Bethnal Green way. But the city's growing, see, and landlords want the land for 'ouses. More money in it. So we 'ad to go. Thought it would be better for Lizzie any rate – after Esther and ev'ryfing." Spencer continued, "Funny fing is, if y' walks up by the nursery on the uvver side of the road there's whoppin' great lines of bricks in the brick fields. Prob'ly won't be long before they takes the nursery too. 'Spect you've seen the fields where they're testin' the land for the right type of clay."

Robert recalled his first evening, thinking London farmers were a poor lot. Not mismanaged fields then, but test sites for the brick manufacturers. "We grew our vegetables too, when I was a lad," Robert recollected his childhood days in Westmorland. "But it was mainly sheep in our area – sheep for the wool trade."

"We grew the lot, between us. Uncles with fruit trees, apples and pears mostly. Grandparents had flowers, dahlias and roses and fruit like raspberries and strawberries – all for them uppish houses back west. Father and me, we did the beans and carrots and suchlike. At least we was never short of a good meal!"

"Were Lizzie's family gardeners too?," Robert asked.

"Lord no! They was silk weavers in Spitalfields. 'Er fam'ly come over from France, way back. Summink to do with religion. 'Er real name's Elisabeth-Marie but I says to 'er, Lizzie's good enough for me if I'm good enough for you! And it stuck.

"Silk was a good trade 'til the Acts fixed their wages. Was supposed to be a good thing but then demand fell. Cotton cloth could be bought cheaper and was the rage. The Masters was forbidden to reduce the weavers' pay so they just stopped employin' 'em."

This all sounded very familiar to Robert; hadn't the same thing happened to the wool weavers in the north?

"This was before she was born but 'er parents told 'er stories of how bad it was then; riots, thousands out of work and their looms were left to rot. All that skill wasted! Worse than that, there was people starving, dying in their beds, such as they was. People in such straits that they just 'ad to leave. Lord knows what 'appened to 'em."

"And Lizzie's family?"

"Both parents taken by fever. But 'er brothers was lucky. …Would you call it 'lucky'? What they've been frough! They survived somehow and now those Acts is all gone they can get paid for what their work's worth. You should see some of the stuff they can make! Beautiful it is. Beautiful!" Spencer stressed the word with such pride, Robert sensed there was a great deal of relief and hope for the future.

By now Primrose was riding on Spencer's shoulders and Robert was carrying the leeks. They had been so deep in conversation Robert hadn't noticed how far they had walked. They had passed some grand houses and gardens but now the rows of properties were shabby and run-down. The smell of the land with cows and horses and cabbages had changed to something more unpleasant. Robert drew his coat closer around him. But it wasn't against the cold.

"'Ere we are." Spencer stopped at a door which had long-since lost its coat of paint. He opened the door and was met by a rush of warmth and family. The room was even more poorly furnished than Spencer's back in Hackney but somehow they had decorated it with the customary greenery of the season and despite their obvious poverty there was a wealth of love within the household.

******

The day passed in merriment and feasting, well what passed for feasting in that part of London. Spencer's mother had been busy weeks ago making mincemeat for pies and a plum pudding. The pudding was wrapped in a cloth and was now boiling in a pot on the range to heat it up again. A pork stew was bubbling quietly in a pan and the family's vegetables completed the meal. Ale was flowing freely and singing and telling tall (and sometimes lewd) stories kept everyone entertained. Lizzie looked concerned at some of the language being used, even by her mother-in-law, but Primrose was oblivious to its meaning and was just enjoying the warmth of the fire and the happy atmosphere.

As the day turned to evening, Spencer took down an old fiddle from its place on the wall and started playing. Everyone took their turn at starting a song and Robert taught them one from his childhood:

> *O where are you going to, my pretty little dear,*
> *With your red rosie cheeks, and your coal*
> *black hair?*
> *I'm going a-milking, kind sir, she answered me*
> *And it's strawberry leaves makes the milk-*
> *maids fair….*

Lizzie said it reminded her of *Where are you going to my pretty maid?*, so they sang that version too.

Eventually it was time to make the cold trek back to Hackney. Spencer's mother wrapped a parcel of leftover food in a cloth and, with a hint of tears in her eyes, gave her son a hug as they made their farewells. Spencer bundled Primrose in a shawl (she had fallen asleep long ago) and fixed her on Lizzie's back with the shawl tied securely around her shoulders and waist. Frost glistened on the road, and the soles of their boots crackled on the ground as they walked. Quiet but happy.

"It's time we let the public see the benefits of travelling by steam coach." John Cooper was addressing a small gathering of engineers at his works. "I have great plans for *Journeyman* and her successors. One day we will all travel between towns on steam coaches; horse-drawn coaches will be a thing of the past! I know we have our denigrators in the newspapers – steam is dangerous, engines explode, carriages slip on hills and icy roads, it's a fashion that will soon pass – I've heard it all. We must overcome these obstacles. We know our engine is safe. We know *Journeyman* causes less damage to muddy road surfaces than horses' hooves and carriages' narrow wheels. If nothing else, the atrocious weather of the past few months has showed that steam carriages can contend with the appalling state of the roads better than horses. Now we must prove she can tackle hills and ice." He paused to emphasise the moment, "We must demonstrate that steam locomotion is no passing fashion, it is the future!"

The engineers murmured in agreement, and, enthused by the speech, waited for the announcement.

"My ambition is to run a regular service of transport, available to every member of the paying public. We will start by running *Journeyman* through the city. We'll bedeck her with bunting so that she is a sight to behold (as if her very presence wasn't sufficient). We'll let people see her, get used to her being safe on the road, and make them inquisitive for what steam coach travel feels like. We will not run without passengers, I have many acquaintances eager just to ride on her – and willing to pay for the privilege – this will show the mob that it can be done. Eventually, we'll run a regular route through the city – we'll come to details later – and in time, we will set up a regular service to the provinces; Bath perhaps, or York."

These were ambitious plans; the engineers began to discuss the implications. Cooper continued, "But. But one *Journeyman* is not enough. We need to build at least two more to start with, and eventually a whole …" he struggled to find the word, "stable full!"

Everyone had questions and ideas to put forward. Cooper held up his hand to quieten them, pleased that his men were with him and as eager to progress as he was. "I'll call you in to my office to discuss details of your responsibilities. Meanwhile, continue with your tasks and think about how we can make this work."

******

Cooper had a flourishing foundry. He made ironworks for horse-drawn carriage- and cart-makers and for canal boats. He was never short of orders. But the steam carriage experiment was an expensive venture and he knew he needed more capital to proceed. He kept his concerns from his men but knew he must set up a company to draw in investors. What should he call it? *Cooper's Steam Carriage Company"*? No, too vague. *Cooper's London Steam Carriage Company*? It must convey his vision of the future. *Cooper's London and Provincial Steam Carriage Company*? A bit of a mouthful, but the best he could think of for now.

He contacted his bank and made plans to hold a meeting to recruit investors. He arranged for a meeting to be held in a hall in Holborn and put advertisements in the newspapers.

He set about employing more workers for the foundry, to build the new carriages and worked with the engineers to make plans for improvements to *Journeyman* to make her lighter and even more reliable. He even charged two of his brightest young employees to investigate where the roads bustled with crowds travelling to and from work in the city, where they went, and the times that the streets were busiest. If that meant being out and about at five or six o'clock in the morning, or until seven at night, then that was their duty. He didn't envisage his clientele as being the well-off with their own carriages, nor those who could easily afford to hire a hackney coach. Nor did he expect to get any business from the lower orders who frequented the eastern part of the city and "get what employment they can at the docks or by base criminality". He was hoping to engage with the 'middling sort', the clerks and secretaries of the offices in the city, the servants of the better coaching inns and up-and-coming hotels, and perhaps on Saturday and Sunday afternoons he could run excursions to Hampstead or Highgate, or even Greenwich.

Over the following months Robert, Walter and even John Cooper himself, took *Journeyman* around the streets of the capital. Cooper ensured there was always a full load of twelve passengers, even if they were employees, family or friends who had ridden many times before. Choosing to go when the streets were crowded, they were never without an audience. On two occasions they made long-distance journeys, not as far as Bath or York, but once to Reading and once to Canterbury.

Unfortunately, the drivers of the horse-drawn carriages were antagonistic towards the new type of vehicle. For once, hackney drivers and their superior (so they thought) associates, private coach drivers, found a common voice, decrying the steam carriage, saying it was dangerous and out of control. Either through fear of losing their own trade or just because it was a novelty, they would drive too close to the *Journeyman* or even get three or four fellow drivers to surround her and stop her from moving. It was reckless behaviour as the constant swerving and close contact would not only unsettle the horses, but on more than one occasion, almost cause the horse-carriage to tip over – bumping and endangering the passengers inside.

Cooper was so enraged by this reckless and backward-looking conduct he had a letter published in the *London Courier* and the *Times* describing what he had seen.

> ..... On one of the excursions, on a busy section of road near Kings Cross, *Journeyman* was close behind a hackney coach. A young boy ran across the road immediately in front of the hackney. The driver swerved but hit the boy and knocked him to the ground. The pilot of *Journeyman* immediately perceived the danger and so instantaneously stopped the vehicle as to prevent further mischief and injury to the boy. A pair of horses, under the same circumstances, could scarcely have failed to aggravate it.

Realising that letters to newspapers effectively gave him free advertising, Cooper became a regular correspondent, and on another occasion wrote:

> ..... Another recurring topic for the naysayers of steam transport is the impossibility of a steam carriage ascending steep hills. I can report with utmost certainty that they can. On a particular day this month *Journeyman* was driven to Pentonville-hill (a rise of approximately 1 in 18). A severe frost frost succeeding a shower of sleet, had completely glazed the road, so that horses could scarcely keep their footing. *Journeyman,* however, did her duty nobly and the hill was ascended at considerable speed, and its summit successfully attained, while the carriages with horses were still but a little way from the bottom.

The trials had proved to Cooper that steam carriages were safe, did not cause inconvenience or alarm to horses, and could traverse the roads of London with ease. Travelling further afield was fraught with problems though.

"It is of great tribulation," Cooper confessed to Robert and Walter, "that a journey of thirty miles or so, which could be concluded far quicker than by conventional carriage, was delayed by petty problems such as having to send a boy with a cart to fetch coke, and use a duck pond to supply water! It makes the experiments a laughing stock. We need to ensure that stations are established along the roads where supplies can be furnished. Of course, it is more expense but as steam transport becomes the norm, perhaps we can work with other steam carriage builders and share stations in some way."

"That is not the only obstacle to progress," Walter added. "I have read that there is great consternation in the equine community that horses will become a thing of the past. Some stabling establishments are fearing their demise. Although they claim to be protecting the jobs of stable boys, farmers growing oats and so on, I think it is their own livelihoods they are looking to protect. Why, there have even been occasions when deep grit has been spread across the way to deliberately impede a steam carriage's progress. Grit that could have been put to better use repairing the ubiquitous holes and divots, in my opinion!"

Robert added further concerns. "The Turnpike Trusts are demanding ridiculously high tolls. How can they justify twelve times that required from a carriage drawn by four horses? We have shown time and again that our vehicles cause less damage to the road surface than a lumbering horse-drawn carriage with its narrow wheels and abrading horses' hooves."

"Yes, yes", Cooper interrupted. "It is deplorable how progress and innovation is stalled and challenged by those who have little knowledge and rely on rumour for their opinions. But we *can* overcome the challenges. We will continue with our work. I am in no doubt that steam travel *is* the future."

As the years passed Robert and Spencer became great friends, and Lizzie regarded him as part of their little family. Spencer was proud to pass on his market gardening knowledge and the two men competed good-naturedly to grow the finest vegetables their meagre plot allowed. Their constant work on the plot was gradually improving the soil and each year the harvest seemed to improve. Lizzie insisted they made room for flowers "and me lit'le bi' o' thyme 'n ros-emry". She adored the colours in her small patch of primroses and violets that she had "saved from the cartwheels" when she surreptitiously removed them from a roadside one springtime.

But growing vegetables was no better than working to Spencer and fishing had become his favourite pastime. When other obligations allowed, Spencer and Robert went off to the Lea. The banks were often crowded with others eager to fish; some for sport, some for the pot, some to show off their new tackle, and others just to spend time with a good companion or in solitude.

It was early morning and the river bank was quiet, the water still and bright. The men carefully baited their hooks and cast their lines. They hoped to catch a pike or perch for a good fish dinner. "Don't bring me no pike," Lizzie had warned, "All them blasted bones!"

As they sat waiting for some response from the river, Robert recalled his childhood days in the fells of Westmorland, and fishing in the becks and burns. He described the exhilaration of tickling his first trout.

"You get to know the river; it's calm edges and its swift channels. You also learn the trout's favourite spots to lay and wait for a passing morsel of food. So, starting downstream," he lowered his voice to add to the mystery, "you inch towards where you think a trout will be. It's there! You've spotted the movement as it darts for quarry and back again. Now, you lay in the water, you become the river. No sound, no movement or shadow to fright the fish. He's busy watching upstream, you get right behind him – the slightest wrong move and he'll be gone. Still your breath and cautiously, like a frond of weed, brush the fish under the tail. Gradually, gradually, tickle your way along the fish's side, increasing the degree of contact. Don't be in a rush. Become the fish; sense its unease and pull back a little. When the time is right, slide your hand under its belly and rubbing gently forwards and backwards, move your hand forwards. Now your hand is embracing under the fish's body. The fish is locked in awe."

Spencer was in awe too, holding his breath so as not to lose the fish. The two men were bent over, head-to-head, in pursuit of the trout.

"Your hand is close to the gills. A swift thrust of finger tips, a tighter grasp, and …… it's yours!" Robert swung upwards raising his hands with the imaginary fish. His voice changed. "It's yours but you've tricked it, you sought its confidence and betrayed it. To catch a fish with hook and bait is one thing, the fish can perhaps see the danger and avoid it. We are using it's feeding habits for our benefit and inventing ever new ways to gain an advantage. But tickling a fish is something different; it's far from this remote game of cat and mouse."

With that, Robert stood up and recast his line, trying downstream this time, and drawing the bait back towards him. He needed to re-focus for a moment. He was looking forward to eating a good dish of fried perch.

Robert's attention was drawn back to Spencer, "Are you all right?" Spencer was staring blankly into the water, but Robert could tell his mind wasn't on the illusive fish. "Yeah, yeah, I'm jus' finking abaht Primrose."

"She's not poorly, is she?"

"No, no, nothing like that. It's just that she...," Spencer paused, uncertain how to continue. He really did not want to say this, even to his friend. "She starts at the school soon."

"Is that causing such concern?" Robert thought. Surely Spencer should be pleased that a place has been found for her. "Is it Lizzie? Is she worried about her being away from her for the first time? Or is it the cost of new boots? I would be happy to buy her some new ones." Robert regretted saying that as soon as the words left his mouth. He hoped he hadn't seemed to be condescending; the wealthy lodger vaunting his greater income to give charity to his poor landlord.

"No, not that, in fact with Primmy at school, Lizzie can find work and improve our lot a little. No, it's just that..." again he paused, trying to find the right words, "Well, Primmy will be learning 'er letters and such, and will ask us things, and we..., we won't be able to 'elp."

A second's thought and Robert realised: Spencer and Lizzie can't read or write. He scanned the house in his mind – no, there are no books other than his own. In fact, the only writing he had ever seen in the house was the notice in their window on that first evening. Again he spoke before thinking, "But how did you write the advertisement you put in your window?"

Spencer blushed a little. "That were Mr Elkins, m'guvn'rs idea. Said it would get us some extra income. 'E wrote it for me."

Picking his words carefully this time, Robert continued, "Can I help, perhaps? Not just with Primrose though, I can show you too – if you'd like me to."

Spencer looked up. It did seem a good idea. He didn't know if Lizzie would need to learn but he thought it would be good for him to find out how to read. "But yer a busy man, Robert. I don't want to take up y' time."

"It's no trouble, I'm happy to do it. It's settled. We can start as soon as you like." They returned to their fish, or lack of them. They pulled in their lines, re-baited the hooks and cast them out again. "Actually," Robert started, "There's something I'd like you to do for me."

"What's that?"

"There's a tunnel being dug under the Thames." Spencer looked at him, puzzled. "I know it sounds ridiculous, doesn't it? I heard about it years ago when I first came to London. I didn't believe it either." He felt there was no need to explain that he didn't believe it because it was intelligence passed to him by a seasoned liar. "Well, it's true and they are digging from Rotherhithe to Wapping. They're letting people in to see it being done. The method sounds ingenious and I fancy going to look. Would you come with me? It's a different sort of digging to what you're used to!"

"A tunnel *under* the Thames. Sounds dangerous to me. We don't 'ave to go in it do we?"

"Oh yes, you go right under the river. It's perfectly safe. Even ladies have been down there. Will you come?"

"Well, alright," Spencer replied uncertainly, "An' I s'pose Wapping isn't far from Bethnal Green, we could all walk to muvver's an' leave Lizzie and Primmy there. Wouldn't take no more than an hour."

"Unfortunately, they've started at the other end, we'd have to go to Rotherhithe. I'll pay for the hackney though." Robert hoped he didn't sound like the benevolent uncle again. He thought he'd best not mention the shilling entrance fee to see the tunnel.

******

So it was, that a few days later Spencer found himself riding in a hackney coach with Robert. He'd never ridden in one before and it wasn't nearly as grand as he had supposed. The carriage rattled and rocked over the cobbles and its passengers were jolted and jostled as the driver manoeuvred through the traffic. The noise was not much deadened by the, what Spencer assumed had once been quite sumptuous, upholstery which was now worn and threadbare with disconcerting dark patches. There was also a distinct odour. Spencer detected stale tobacco and sweat but there was something else he couldn't quite pinpoint. He began to feel a little sick and wondered why he'd agreed to this adventure with Robert. He looked out of the window – so many people and carriages rushing from here to there. He smiled to himself as he thought if people just decided to live on the opposite sides of the city, would there be such need for everyone to travel?

The carriage continued to negotiate the narrow streets of the city. "We're about to cross the river." Robert informed him. "Now, look to your right. This is history in the making."

As they crossed the Thames, just a few yards to the west, were dozens of men working on a new bridge. Great wooden tripods formed cranes to lower men and rocks from the working platform to the sides of massive stone arches being constructed across the river. A lacy frame of timbers supported each arch which stretched from newly built piers in the river. Some arches were almost complete while others were still in the early stages. There was great activity around one particular arch where it looked as if the keystone was being prepared to be lowered into its final position.

Spencer cursed the passing carriages that kept obscuring his view.

"It's the new London Bridge. Another of Rennie's design," Robert told him. He is getting quite a reputation as a bridge designer in London – and beyond."

"Why do they need another bridge so close to this one?" Spencer wondered.

"Ah, this will be knocked down when the new one is complete. It's too narrow you see, for all the traffic."

Spencer agreed the bridge they were on did seem very congested.

"A bridge has stood here for hundreds of years. It's been altered a bit, of course, but it's time for it to go. That's what I meant by 'history in the making. This old bridge will be here no longer." Robert continued, pleased to have a receptive audience. "They're hoping the new bridge will stop the river freezing too. The wide spans of the arches will let the river flow more freely. It's another reason to demolish this one, and get rid of its foundations."

The carriage arrived at the south side of the river and turned east. Within another quarter of an hour they reached their destination. Robert paid the driver and the two friends joined the people in the street. Spencer was dazzled by the sight he now saw. A bright stone rotunda stood before them with people coming and going. Robert paid the fee to enter and they began to descend a long, long winding staircase. Instead of a narrow dingy tunnel that Spencer had expected, the shaft was light and airy and lit by gas lamps.

"Isn't it magnificent!" Robert breathed.

Spencer was a little concerned that they were descending so far into the ground. "Are you sure it's safe?"

At the bottom of the stairs they came into a chamber, not of one tunnel but two, side-by-side. The gravelled walkway was peppered with sight-seers walking and talking and admiring the massive structure. Voices echoed eerily in the brick-lined tunnel which seemed to continue forever under the river.

"We can't get to the Wapping side yet," Robert told him, but we can walk a good way under the river."

Spencer walked with him, nervously glancing at the ceiling, hoping not to spot any signs of water leaking in.

"It's a very clever way of tunnelling, never been tried before." This didn't make Spencer feel any better.

"They have a cage," he showed Spencer a picture in the booklet he had bought at the ticket office. "See, the men stand in their own little space and dig away at the clay. When they have all dug a foot or so, the cage is pushed forward to the face of the clay and the exposed side-walls are bricked solid. Clever, eh?"

Spencer thought about it. "A bit like an earthworm eating through the soil?" The method interested him, but a feeling of foreboding would not disappear. He was glad when Robert suggested they returned to the surface.

Back on firm ground, Spencer's normal chirpiness returned. "A new bridge and a tunnel! The English are great engineers, no doubt about that!"

"Well, Rennie's Scottish and Brunel is French – but I take the point. We are not afraid of trying out new engineering."

Primrose skipped along, beside her father as he walked with her to school. Lizzie wasn't feeling well so Spencer had offered to take her on his way to work. Primrose had taken to schooling well, had settled in and made friends. The schoolmistress reported she was willing and obedient – and that was all you ask for, her anxious parents thought.

Primrose did enjoy being at school, although she was a little frightened of the older children who appeared so much bigger than her and could be intimidating at times. The big boys, especially, seemed to like to fight, although they never threatened Primrose or her friends; in fact, they barely noticed the little ones at all. Primrose had made a friend of another little girl, Maisie. They sat next to each other on the bench at the front of the school-room. They would sit up with straight backs and folded arms when Miss Cameron, the schoolmistress came into the room, just as they had been instructed. The boys behind them took great delight at pulling their hair ribbons and even their hair, to make them squeal and get a telling off. The girls would then do their best to get revenge by making the boys giggle when they should be listening in silence.

The school day always started with prayers and a story from the bible. Primrose didn't always understand what the stories were about but she enjoyed Miss Cameron's 'story-telling' voice. Both boys and girls were taught the alphabet and reading. They practised writing letters on a slate with a pencil also formed from slate. Primrose frequently had her knuckles rapped because she was holding the pencil incorrectly – after which she would 'accidently' scrape the slate awkwardly, producing an ear-piercing screech which caused Miss Cameron to shudder visibly.

In the afternoons the boys were taught separately and learnt arithmetic, while the girls were shown how to master the skills of needlework. The curriculum was laid down by the subscribers to the school, who, for forty shillings a year, could demonstrate their philanthropic propensity. However, Miss Cameron was eager to go beyond their prescriptive ideas. She would often bring flowers or shells into the schoolroom, and a bird's nest with eggs on one occasion. She would talk about the objects with the children and let them examine them. She liked to let the children talk about their own experiences related to the object on show. Primrose gave a very enlightening talk on using certain products as plant nourishment when Miss Cameron produced a marrow one day.

******

Taking Primrose to school had diverted Spencer from his usual route and he found himself walking past a little huddle of businesses. One had assorted joints of meat hanging in front of its window and across the doorway, another offered a meagre range of vegetables arranged on a window-ledge that served as a shelf, and another had buckets and brushes and all kinds of household goods for sale, but what caught Spencer's eye was a colourful display of bolts of fabric behind unusually clean small-paned windows. He paused to have a closer look. "Ow Lizzie would love to 'ave a frock made from that," he thought to himself, and smiled, regretfully knowing it would be impossible to purchase such a fine cotton. Then he noticed a small card wedged in the cross-timbers of the window. Before Robert had started to teach him to read, Spencer would have ignored such a thing, but now he slowly spelled the writing out to himself:

S E A M S T R E S S

He broke the word down into sounds he recognised, just as Robert had shown him. "ess, tress … sea, seam … Seamstress!" The next word was more difficult but he guessed they needed a seamstress. Lizzie must have seen the notice when she came this way to buy the odd thing, but she would not have realised what it said. He must tell her this evening – it would be an ideal position for her, now that Primrose is at school.

******

When Spencer returned home from work that evening, he was relieved to find Lizzie well and Primrose playing happily. Lizzie was full of apologies for having made Spencer take Primrose to school and explained that she felt recovered by dinner time and was able to fetch her herself. Truly she felt a fraud for having complained at all – it wasn't like Lizzie not to shrug off feeling under the weather.

"Never mind that," Spencer reassured her, "It might 'ave been our good luck." He explained about the notice in the draper's window and they both agreed the additional income would be very welcome.

"I know where y' mean. I've often looked in the window – lovely stuff, dunno 'oo can afford it round 'ere though." She thought for a second. "When Primrose is a'bed I'll sort frough some sewing I've got – all a bit tatty now though I s'pose."

******

And so, the next morning Lizzie and Primrose set off on the usual route to school, but this time Lizzie had a bundle of samples of the stitching she could do to show the proprietor of the draper's shop. She had sat up late into the night sewing fine neat stiches by the meagre light of the oil lamp – "Better than candlelight", she mused as she sewed, "and them old things is no good to show off."

"What's up, ma?" Primrose sensed Lizzie's unease and hoped she wasn't poorly again.

"Nuffin', Primmy love," she smiled at her daughter's concern, "Just a few collywobbles."

The notice was still in the window, so Lizzie took a deep breath and pushed the door open. A bell jingled loudly and Lizzie's nerves rose another notch. The room smelled of fresh fabric, several bolts of which were stacked regularly on stout wooden shelves behind a long polished wooden counter. Displays of ribbon and buttons gave the shop a welcoming feel and Lizzie warmed to the unfamiliar surroundings. As she reached the counter, a middle-aged woman appeared from a doorway that led to the back rooms.

"Good morning, how can I help you today?"

Lizzie stammered her reply. She had practised it all the way from school, and every time she had stirred in her sleep last night.

"I'm, … I've… I", her heart sank, not a good start. "I believe you need a seamstress," she nodded towards the window, and continued in her 'best' voice, "I 'ave good hexperience, lots of hexperience. I've made dozens of dresses and such, an' can do all sorts hov stitching."

The woman smiled and Lizzie relaxed a little. "And have you brought some things to show me?" She indicated the bundle, now tightly held in Lizzie's hands.

"Hoh, yes." Lizzie spilled the samples onto the counter. How shabby they looked in the light of day.

The woman picked them up and examined each one closely. "This is very fine work, indeed." she declared approvingly. Lizzie almost beamed but was aware she still didn't yet have the job. "You are well-trained, I can see that. But you have not worked for a while?" The woman guessed as much from the lack of new material. She could tell that it was newly sewn but the fabric had seen better days long ago.

Lizzie explained her background and why she had not been able to work recently. She almost told the story of losing Hester, but stopped herself, thinking it would sound too desperate, and theirs wasn't such an unusual tale anyway.

"Well, we have been searching for a while but I think today we may have found who we are looking for. Come through to the back and meet Mr Cross."

"Vince, duck, 'ere's the girl we need." Lizzie started at the woman's sudden change of voice as she dropped her 'deferential serve the customer' façade and reverted to her real self. An hour later,

Lizzie left the shop. Mr and Mrs Cross had given her the job. She would work every day, except Saturdays and Sundays, in a room above the shop. They would give her repairs to do to start with, "to see 'ow we all get along" and then, she hoped, they would employ her to make finer garments for the clients they claimed they had in the city.

"Just a little back-water for now," Vincent Cross confided, "but one day, we'll have premises in the finest street in town!"

Back-water or not, Lizzie didn't care – she had a job!

******

Lizzie followed Mrs Cross up a steep stairway to a room over the shop. It was larger than Lizzie expected. One wall was taken up with shelves stacked with paste-board crates and packages, the opposite wall had a fireplace and small grate and the alcoves were filled with two matching chests of drawers. The room faced the back of the property; it had a large window that looked out over a neglected courtyard. Lizzie noticed a stone-built outhouse in one corner of the yard.

"Is that the privy?" she asked.

"Lawd no! You've no business in there." Mrs Cross's mouth twitched as it always did when she thought she'd said something amusing. "Necessary's down an alley two doors down." she indicated the direction along the road.

In front of the window was a mahogany table and two old dining chairs that were past their days of glory. A mannequin stood in one corner, sporting an elegant green taffeta gown, with a lace trimming that was partly attached. Lizzie hoped she'd be given the task to finish.

"This is where we work," Mrs Cross nodded towards the chairs, "All the cottons and notions are in them drawers. Mind y' keep 'em tidy. I'll be 'ere some days, but some days you'll be on y'r own." Anxious not to waste precious working time, she produced some garments from one of the boxes. They all seemed to be undergarments that needed some kind of repair.

"Simple stuff to start," Mrs Cross said abruptly, "We'll see 'ow y' go."

Lizzie was to be paid by the piece, and mending seams and sewing buttons wasn't going to earn her much, but she set to work willingly.

Mrs Cross returned downstairs. Lizzie went to the drawers and searched for the tools she needed. They were indeed very well organised. "I'll never remember what goes in each drawer," she thought. She decided to leave the drawers slightly ajar, so at least she'd find the right ones again. She sat at the table, turning her chair to face the light. The courtyard was unpaved, plain and empty apart from a few old wooden crates and some barrels. It was surrounded by high walls with a large gateway out to a track that ran behind the properties. The outhouse had a solid wooden door, and ivy and other greenery clambered up the walls and over the slate roof like fingers of nature trying to reclaim their rightful place.

After working for a couple of hours, Lizzie stretched her back and sat away from her work. She could do with finding the privy. As she went down the stairs, she could hear the murmur of a conversation between the Crosses and another gentleman. She paused at the doorway to the back room to explain where she was going. In a split second the conversation stopped, the stranger turned his head so she could not see his face and Mrs Cross looked up with a fixed expression, before it melted into a smile. Lizzie felt she had intruded on something private and scuttled to the door of the shop. The bell rang loudly and jangled her nerves once again. She pulled the door tight shut behind her.

It was raining now, so Lizzie drew her shawl up over her head and walked the few yards to the alleyway. The upper storeys of the buildings were joined, making a little tunnel and a bit of respite from the rain. In the yard at the back of the buildings stood an outhouse with two doors. She opened the first and found it was the entrance to the wash-house with a copper, now sitting cold in one corner. On opening the second door the stench knocked her back a pace. With no other option, she held one hand over her nose and mouth and lifted her skirts out of the grime with the other

"At least it's a one-seater," she thought to herself – though that was really of little comfort.

No more than two months had passed before Lizzie realised she was going to have a baby again.

"Me courses 'aven't come," she confided to Spencer one evening. "I reckon there's a littl'un on the way."

They both shared the joy and apprehension of the news. Joy, of course, in welcoming a new member of the family, but apprehension about whether it would be taken by illness, how they could afford to feed and clothe another child, and how they would all live together in their little house with Robert taking up one room.

"I know we're better off than lots," Lizzie said "Some's livin' ten to a room, I know that. But I'm scared, Spence, I don't mind tellin' yer."

"Don't fret luv," Spencer tried to comfort her, but the same feelings were running through his head too. "We'll sort sumfin. Let's be 'appy, eh?"

******

Lizzie said nothing to her employers, whose trust she was just beginning to earn. Mrs Cross (she was always called 'Mrs Cross', even by her husband) had started to give her more meaningful tasks. She was working on a sumptuous silk evening gown and casually wondered who could afford such a garment. She knew Vince often made visits to the city, so she guessed he must have some well-to-do contacts there.

Mrs Cross had also entrusted some very expensive lace tuckers and trims to her for repair or for attaching to sleeves and bodices. Mrs Cross was quite an expert when it came to lace and taught Lizzie how to distinguish between true Honiton bobbin lace and the foreign made laces, although she admitted Brussels lace was of high quality. Some patterns she could recognise as being from particular regions, and she could tell whether a machine-made net used as ground for the finer work had been manufactured in Nottingham or France!

As the winter took hold and the room grew colder, Lizzie asked if she could light a fire in the grate. Mrs Cross's reply was disheartening. "I really thought you 'ad more sense! What's the smoke goin' to do to these fine white fabrics – not to mention the smell they'll take on. No fires but y' can 'ave a dick-pot with coals from the fire downstairs."

Lizzie was grateful for the little earthenware pot to put on the floor beneath her skirts. The warmth from the hot coals helped to keep the blood flowing in her feet and legs. She also brought extra shawls and made little cotton fingerless gloves to help her through the coldest days, but she went home with red and painful fingers almost every day.

The weeks and months passed and Lizzie gradually loosened her corsets little-by-little. Spring returned, and it was soon going to be difficult to conceal her condition from the Crosses any longer. "They will 'ave to know sometime," she thought, "Best to get it over wiv."

Ever able to surprise, they didn't seem at all concerned. "You fink we 'adn't noticed!" Vince teased, "You just keep going, love. When y'r liitl'un's born you can work at 'ome – not on the good stuff though, mind."

It had lifted a worry from Lizzie's shoulders and every day seemed a little brighter. As she sat at the table with her needle and thread, she would often gaze aimlessly into the courtyard. She was sure the barrels and crates moved about, but they were always old-looking, as if they had been there for years. "Just a silly fancy," she guessed. One day her attention was taken by movement in the greenery over the outhouse. She watched for a while and saw it was a robin darting in and out, coming and going. She realised there must be a nest and followed the bird's progress over the weeks. Some days he was busy bringing beakfuls of grubs or something, other times he would sit on the highest point of the roof and sing loudly. It was the most joyful sound she could imagine.

******

Later that summer Lizzie recognised the starting pains of childbirth. Spencer went to fetch the midwife and Lizzie assured him she would be all right until he returned.

After some thirty minutes, he was back with Mrs Lucas. He looked anxiously at Robert when he opened the door.

"She's fine," Robert said. "She's been moaning a bit but says she's all right. I listened at the door and shouted through." Robert's voice tailed off, as he recognised his complete inadequacy for the situation.

Mrs Lucas was a diminutive woman, small-framed and not much over five foot tall. But what she lacked in stature she made up for in her forthright authoritarian manner. One glance at the men and then she was up the stairs without further invitation.

Barely ten minutes later she was down again. The men looked at her expectantly. "Surely it can't be all over yet?" Robert thought. Then a moment's panic as he could hear no baby crying.

"Nothing 'appn'ng for a while yet," she said. "I'll be back later and we'll see what's to do."

Spencer went up to his wife. She said she'd stay in bed for a while but welcomed his offer of 'a nice cuppa tea'.

When Mrs Lucas returned, with no other option, Spencer and Robert kept well out of the way. Spencer hated hearing the yowls from the room upstairs and reassured Primrose that there was nothing to worry about "It's all as it should be," he told her, though he was far from confident.

Lizzie's pains were growing stronger and more

frequent. Mrs Lucas talked soothingly and encouragingly to Lizzie. She had been at the births of countless babies and little flustered her, but she knew Lizzie was in for a hard time. The baby was breech and delivering him would be challenging for all three of them. She steeped some herbs in the hot water she had asked Spencer to bring, and gave Lizzie a cup to sip the infusion from.

The strong pains had continued for more than two hours. Lizzie gripped the iron bedstead and was weak from effort and frustration. Without showing her concerns, Mrs Lucas examined Lizzie again. The baby was coming, but it wasn't his head she could see. She would need to help him into the world, and it was going to take all her skills. She encouraged Lizzie off the bed and to kneel up against it. Lizzie obeyed blindly. The pains came again. She rested her head in her hands and her thoughts drifted. She was aware she had a body but somehow it didn't belong to her. Mrs Lucas was doing something; she was too tired to even think about what was happening. She felt faint and dizzy. She could see pictures of pretty white flowers in her head. They were in Primrose's hair. She was grown and wearing a long white dress.

They were walking close by a river where some white ducks were swimming alongside. The ducks were quacking "Quack! Quack!" They continued "Quaack! Quaack!" "Quaack! Quaack!" Someone was calling her "Lizzie, Lizzie, tuppence, Lizzie." Mrs Lucas helped her back onto the bed. The quacking changed. Lizzie realised it was a baby crying. Mrs Lucas handed her a bundle. "You have a son," she said softly. Now all Lizzie's thoughts were focused on the warm scrap of life, suckling at her breast. His long body and legs seemed to embrace her and his fingers wrapped themselves tightly around one of hers. Mrs Lucas was still doing something. She didn't know what. She was too tired to think.

"William," she said to herself, "After Spencer's father… And Robin… William Robin Taylor."

11

1829

J Cooper Esq. was extremely irked at having had to enlist share-holders: they would be taking a portion of *his* profits. But it was the only way he could raise enough capital to carry his ambitious project forward.

Testing and improvements to the carriage's design meant he now had a new model called *London Clipper* (he liked the nautical allusion and felt the name conveyed speed and comfort). The latest *Clipper* had the body of the carriage and the engine suspended independently on improved leaf springs, and the body had a roof to protect the passengers from all but the worst of weather. Although not the original intention, Cooper realised that roof could also be employed as space for luggage and goods that needed transporting across the city, as well as outside seating if required, in the manner of a long-distance horse-carriage. The new *Clippers* could also carry twenty passengers, instead of the original twelve on *Journeyman*, as well as a pilot, a fireman, an engineer and a guard. There was also space for water buckets and more than enough coke to complete a journey across the city.

The new carriages would have to be in service very soon. Apart from the drain that all the testing, refinements and worry had put on Cooper's finances and health, the shareholders were getting anxious about not yet having seen any return for their investments. Worse still, rumours were circulating that another engineer was about to commence "omnibus" services in the manner of the French system; these would be horse-drawn carriages. The competition was not welcomed by Cooper but steam carriages did not need to be rested and stabled after half a day's work so he felt he was at an advantage.

He pored over his account books; taking running costs, tolls, costs of repairs, wages and allowances for contingencies into account, he contemplated what to charge his passengers in order to make a good return on the outlay.

John Cooper was proud of continuing the family tradition of being ready to embrace new methods of travel. To him, steam carriages were a natural progression from the horse-drawn variety that had been used for centuries, Some may think him stuffy and pompous, but he considered himself modern and forward-thinking. Always ready to inform others of his shrewd business acumen, he did not shy from proclaiming his achievements when writing to a close friend ….

Journeyman is giving reliable service and with improvements we have constructed three "London Clippers" each being a progression on the earlier models.

I have acquired land and set up a small workshop and base in Fulham. We will run two carriages concurrently, travelling East to West and West to East. We had thought to have passengers hail the carriage in the manner of a hackney coach, but feared this would enrage the hackney drivers unnecessarily, and the constant stopping and starting would be a great annoyance to the other passengers already on the carriage. Instead I have installed boards on convenient walls or in windows (sometimes having to pay the owners an outrageous fee for the privilege!). These authorised stopping places indicate where the carriage will stop and allow our passengers to embark and disembark.

The boards and posters are of my own design, and I think they convey the quality and reliability of the service to be expected. They are surmounted with "London and Provincial Steam Carriage Co" in the same distinctive and distinguished style as adorns my carriages. It is a name that will soon become synonymous with London travel in everybody's mind.

It was with great reluctance that I decided to omit 'Cooper' from the company's name for fear that the vulgar sort will abbreviate it to C.L.A.P.S. Carriages, the connotations of which, you will understand, would bring great injury to my business, my family and myself. .....

He went on to describe the routes the carriages would be taking. Two early-morning carriages would set out, one from Hackney to Fulham, and the other in the opposite direction. They would bring passengers from the outer parts of London (including Paddington and Somers Town) to the city, concentrating on the busy thoroughfares of Holborn, Piccadilly and Westminster, as well as the more residential roads in Mayfair and along the City Road and Oxford Street.

It had taken many long meetings with his senior staff to finalise the details of the plans for running the service. Coke, or at worst London coal, was the fuel of choice as it burned with greater heat efficiency and could be carried on the carriage – extra supplies being available at the "stations" at Hackney and Fulham. Water was easily available in the many horse troughs around the city, but buckets would also be carried on-board. They simplified the system of fares by charging each passenger one shilling, no matter how long they rode for. This enabled the guard to merely collect fares and keep his attention on the safety of the passengers and goods; he didn't have to watch for people riding beyond their entitled destination or remember complicated tables of fare charges. Somebody riding right across the city would have a bargain ride but, they calculated, the majority of people would be taking short journeys. A shilling was cheaper than most Hackney coach fares, but they would be carrying twenty passengers at a time.

******

At last, the day came. The *London and Provincial Steam Carriage Company* was about to launch its first regular service for paying passengers across the spread of the great metropolis. The pilots and guards were smartly dressed (liveried uniforms were an unnecessary expense, Cooper insisted) and wore caps in the same dark green of the carriages and emblazoned with a brass hat badge bearing "PILOT" and "GUARD". (These were the creation of a young apprentice in Cooper's own works, who had been delighted to show off his skills in their making.) The firemen and engineers had been told to "dress appropriately", that is, functional clothing, as smart as possible.

At seven in the morning they drew up at their allotted starting place. To their surprise and delight a small crowd had gathered. Only five passengers actually got on the carriage at Hackney, and only three in Fulham. A disappointing start.

12

1830

After an uncertain beginning to the omnibus service, as it was now officially called, things had significantly improved. The carriages were almost constantly full, particularly "with the petticoat kind" as one pilot described the well-dressed ladies who seemed to make interminable visits to their dressmaker and other acquaintances. They found the carriages comfortable and smooth to ride in, and "the inconvenience of smoke and noise" non-existent.

Excursions by Londoners to the green fields of Hampstead and Greenwich were now established as a popular and regular pastime. Even those who had not ridden out from the city enjoyed a "pleasure trip" on the novel transport around the environs of the heaths.

One of the new routes of the 'Barrels' (a play on Cooper's name and to distinguish them from the rival companies of Shillibeer and Hancock) was to Loddiges' magnificent hot house. It was world-famous and housed rare plants from all around the world. But it was Spencer who suggested the 'whole family', for that was how he regarded Robert now, should go and see it. It had been a wet and miserable summer and the idea came to him after overhearing a conversation between his employer and a local seedsman.

"We could all do wiv a bi' o' cheering up," he announced on a rare sunny Sunday morning. "Why don't we take a walk to Loddiges' place?"

"What, the place with the trees?" Lizzie asked, with not too much enthusiasm.

"You'll like it, Lizzie. There's walks and a great room full of flowers you'll never have seen before." Robert was delighted with the idea. He had heard of the novel way of heating the hothouse with a steam machine, and hoped they might see it.

Later that afternoon, all dressed in their 'Sunday Best', they made the short walk to the Botanical Gardens. Spencer held William's hand as he tottered along, and carried him when he got tired. Lizzie was surprised at how many people were there and held tightly to Primrose's hand – as much for her own comfort as for keeping Primrose on her best behaviour.

"At least this should be safer than our visit to your tunnel," Spencer half-joked. He had never forgotten the feeling of trepidation he'd had in the tunnel, and when the dreadful accident happened in early 1828, he felt even more lucky that they had escaped unharmed.

"Yes, that was terrible," Robert admitted. "So many lives lost. But it could have been worse, I suppose."

"Not for the fam'lies of those lost in mud! Just shows. Y' shouldn't meddle wiv nature."

Primrose bent down and picked up a leaf. She smoothed it between her fingers. It was damp from the rain and felt leathery and bumpy. She traced her fingers along the veins and admired the greens and browns, dark on the top and lighter underneath. "What's this?" she asked, waving it at her mother.

"It's from that tree there," Robert pointed towards an oak. You can tell which tree from the shape of the leaves. Do you see?" He indicated the lobes on the leaf. "Do you know?" he continued, "Our navy ships are made from the wood of trees like that. That's only a baby one – they grow to be much, much bigger."

"If I plant my leaf will it grow into a big oak tree?" Primrose asked.

"No, I'm afraid not. You have to plant the seeds from the tree. They're called acorns. We can look for some, but they probably won't be ready for planting yet."

Still pleased with her find, Primrose carried it carefully. "And what's this? It's all pointy."

"I think that's a type of hawthorn."

"Watch out for the prickles, then," her mother warned. Lizzie knew about hawthorns and had sometimes collected the haws to make a gargle to ward off a sore throat. Primrose instantly decided to torment her little brother by pretending she was going to poke him with the prickly twig.

"You promised I'd see flowers I'd never seen before," Lizzie teased Robert.

"Come on then. let's go to the hothouse."

They made their way around the plantation and to the entrance of the most extraordinary building Lizzie had ever seen. It was huge. The closer they walked, the bigger it became. It was in the shape of an enormous glass tunnel; higher than a house – higher than two houses! Thousands of glass panels held together with a frame that, to Spencer's eye looked far too delicate for the weight of glass it must support. They opened the door and went inside. The first impression was the smell, sweet and pungent. The second was the heat and humidity inside this amazing structure. The third was the green. Everything was green as far as you could see. The adults wandered in awe at the tall palm trees and varieties of ferns and other plants they could not name. In one section was a collection of exotic orchids. Lizzie stood and gazed in wonder. For Primrose, for whom everything was new, the exciting part was spotting the little birds that flitted from tree to tree and she pointed them out to William with delight.

After thirty minutes or so, the humidity was beginning to give Lizzie a headache, and she felt decidedly faint. She didn't want to spoil the afternoon for the others so suggested they found their way to the tea-room, which she had spotted earlier. It seemed the perfect way to end the day.

******

As they made their way home, Robert and Spencer discussed the ingenuity of the heating system and how the glass changed the character of the air inside the glasshouse to enable the exotic plants to be grown.

"That glass'ouse must 'ave cost thousands," Spencer speculated. "They can only afford 'em at the big 'ouses. Y' know we'd like one on Mr Elkins' patch. But they're just too rich for us. We use bell jars to force some plants, but y' can only bring on a few. A glass'ouse would mean we could 'ave early fruits on tomatoes 'n such and make a killin' in the market – but not while glass is so dear. Mr Elkins says that if the tax was taken off the cost'd be less than 'alf as much. Then it might be worth finkin abaht." He walked in silence for while. The bright afternoon turned dull and it started raining again. "It don't seem right do it. We work all our lives an' scrape a livin'. Just so we can feed our fam'lies and pay rent to our landlords. It's all the big fam'lies what own the land round 'ere. So they just collect the money an' get richer while we do all the work an' pay them!"

Robert understood exactly what Spencer meant, even if his logic was a bit naïve. The day-to-day round of work and rare pleasures was sometimes as depressing as this summer had been. But there was nothing anyone could do to change things. Politicians had fine words but there were stronger voices who kept taxes and prices high and baulked at greater Poor Relief. One of his sisters, Sarah, and her family. worn down by poor harvests, poor wages and a bleak future had been lured by the promises of the Canada Company and were about to embark on a journey to Upper Canada. He hoped their optimism wasn't misplaced. Once, he'd been fired by the radical thinkers in Manchester but where had that ended? Tragedy and status quo. Those securing benefits from power and position were not going to give it up easily.

13

Winter 1830-1831

Robert and the family huddled around the grate, wrapped in blankets and getting what little warmth they could from the meagre fire.

"'Ave y' ever known such cold?" Spencer asked, rubbing his fingers to get the circulation going.

"I do remember one bad winter, soon after I went to Manchester." Robert recalled the day when they found the young lad from the canal family. He used to wonder what had happened to him, and remembering him now struck a pang of guilt that he'd long forgotten all about him.

"I dunno 'ow we'll get on. Elkins says there's no use goin' to work – ground's too 'ard and frosts'll get everyfink anyway. 'E says 'is bruvver's fam'ly's got it just as bad. They're in the country somewhere – work the land, or try to. They've got 'ardly no food neiver, an' they're growin' the stuff!"

"It's got to get better soon, hasn't it? When the ice clears from the Thames, the colliers'll be able to dock again and the coal supplies should improve. But I don't know where the food's going to come from, with the roads being so bad as well."

"An' what we goin' to pay for it wiv?" Lizzie murmured, "Spencer ain't got no work 'n I ain't 'eard from the Crosses for weeks."

It was dark and miserable. The fire was growing weaker and more ineffective. The only solution was to go to bed and hope tomorrow would bring a break in the weather. The children were tucked up together to help keep each other warm. A blanket from Spencer and Lizzie's bed was spread over them. Lizzie found all the shawls she could to replace their blanket and they cuddled up close using their body-heat to get them through the night. Robert had long since taken to wearing thick woollen stockings under his nightshirt and draped his coat over the covers. When the water in the kettle allowed, he filled a stone bottle with hot water and warmed the bed a little before he got between the icy sheets.

But the weather did not break. The cold continued. Spencer moped about the house with nothing to do. He got angry when the children squabbled and then felt despair at not being able to provide them with proper food and warmth. He slowly shrank into himself. He stopped shaving and had no enthusiasm for anything. Some days he didn't bother to get out of bed. His appetite had gone and he reckoned the food should go to the children anyway.

Lizzie was getting more and more concerned about him. She needed to find him something to do.

"Spencer, I was won'dring, Can y' take Lizzie to school tomorrow? An' can y' call on the Crosses? See if they've any work for me?"

Spencer was reluctant; being supported by his wife was not his idea of married life. But he went anyway, glad to see something other than the inside of his house. He found he actually enjoyed the walk with Primrose, even though the roads were icy and they had to watch they didn't slip or fall.

"What y' doin' in school? Hope yer a good girl."

Primrose assured her father she was 'a good girl' and told him a little of her days. Miss Cameron made sure the stove in the school room was burning well when the children arrived and did all the 'sitting down' lessons in the mornings. In the afternoons, as the fire dwindled, she encouraged the children to practise marching up and down the room, or jumping on the spot – not to teach them any military skills, just to keep them warm. She urged some of the children to come to school early, when she would give them half a baked potato before the others arrived. She guessed some were not getting much to eat at home. But her most novel achievement had been to acquire several sets of knitting needles and crochet hooks and a supply of yarn. She taught the children to knit and crochet, and they were gradually building a supply of irregularly-shaped squares that would become small shawls for each of them.

Having left Primrose, Spencer walked on until he reached the row of shops where Lizzie's draper's stood. He looked in the window. There were no lights showing but he tried the door. It was locked. "Odd," he thought. He tried it again in case it was stuck. The door was definitely locked. Feeling a little foolish, he looked about him and decided to enquire at the pawnbroker's next-door.

"What! Ain't you 'eard? They was done f' smugglin', mumf's back." The pawnbroker was pleased to be able to relay the juicy tale. "A boat got pulled by the excise men down Dover way.

They soon squealed wiv a promise of sayin' who they'd got the stuff from would make the judge look more kindly on 'em. Well, what d'y' know? They was takin' lace *to* France. An' where d'y' thin they got it from? Our very own Mrs Cross!"

Spencer was stunned. Why hadn't they heard before? "What happened? Did they take 'em?"

"Oh, yeah, took 'em alright. Peelers was 'ere, a-bangin' on the door. 'Bout midnight it was, not long before Christmas. Course, the Crosses knew what was coming, so they tries to 'ook it out the back. Not smart enough though – peelers was waitin' for 'em!"

"And where are they now?"

"Well, last I 'eard, they're at Newgate waitn' for their trial. But that's not the best of it."

"No?"

"No. I 'eard there was loads of stuff, not just the Crosses lace, ten crates they found, an' it was all s'pos'd to go to a Lord Stu..., er... an English ambassador in Paris. All sealed up, it was, cos them types don't 'ave to pay no tax, but..." the pawnbroker paused for effect, and to take a breath, "but 'What do 'e need all that stuff for?' the Frenchies are thinkin'. 'E's already spent a king's ransom on 'is 'ome.' So, they decides to take a look inside. Cor, luv us, they 'ad a surprise. Fabric, leather, posh waistcoats, beer, tobacco and sixteen hundredweight of lace! Well, that don't get there by *accident* does it?"

Spencer shook his head in agreement.

"Course 'ol Lord What-d'ye-call-him says 'e knows nuffin abaht it. An' them in the gentry say 'e's a 'discreet and honourable noble lord' 'n it's an 'hunfortunate intervention' by the Frenchies." The pawnbroker stopped talking for a moment, to confirm his story was making the full impact it deserved. Seeing Spencer was completely enthralled, he continued. "And that's not the end of it. Now what do *our* excise men do wiv stuff they find smuggled into *our* country? Confiscate it, o' course and git the smugglers in the clink. But what 'appens to this lot? Gits sent back to England, on the Lord's orders. An' where is it now? Yer guess is as good as mine – and the English Customs don't know neiver!" Realising he had let the sensationalist subject of the story run away with him, and probably spoken a little freer than he should, the pawnbroker's manner suddenly changed. "Anyway, you buyin' somefin'? If not, I got important business to attend to."

"Ah, no. I was just inquirin' abaht the Crosses. I'll not trouble y' again."

Spencer's step was much lighter as he returned home. What a tale to tell Lizzie and Robert! He did wonder how the pawn broker came to know so much though.

******

Lizzie's pale face turned even whiter on hearing Spencer's story. "Oh my Gawd!", she exclaimed. Her hands twitched and she rubbed her cheek nervously. "Oh my Gawd." she repeated softly. "What are we t'do?"

"What d'y mean, love?" Spencer looked at her anxiously.

"I got their stuff. I got their pins, and needles, an' that big pair o' scissors. An' I got their lace!" The words caught breathlessly in her throat. "What we gonna do?"

"Y' don' need t' worry. No one's comin' after you. The p'lice don' even know abaht yer."

It transpired that the lace Lizzie had in her possession was a piece of trimming, no more than fifteen inches long, and certainly not enough to have her 'taken away' as she feared. "In any case," Spencer assured her, "It's English lace on English soil, so you've done nuffin' wrong."

Lizzie didn't sleep well that night and she was up early the next morning. She riddled the grate and set a fire with a little kindling and a few lumps of coal. Held tightly in one hand was the little piece of lace trimming that had worried her so much. She had had plans to use it as a trim on a frock for Primrose, if she should ever have a piece of fabric to make one again. But now, when she thought about it, her heart quickened and her stomach churned. She watched the fine threads catch fire and light up in flame.

The excursion of the day before had had a positive effect on Spencer. He offered to take Primrose to school again and then resolved to go on to the home of his employer, Henry Elkins.

Henry lived in a small cottage in Lower Clapton. It was one of a row of four single-storey, thatched cottages that had been built many years before for farm labourers. But the farm was slowly shrinking and the cottages were now let to other workers. A shoemaker lived in one end with his wife and five children, next to him was a brick-maker, a widower with two children, then came Henry's cottage and next to him, a carpenter. Henry and his wife had moved there, to be close to his wife's family, more than thirty years ago. They had never had children and now that he was a widower, the nursery and market gardening was all he had. Spencer had been to his cottage only once before, back in '26 or '27, he thought. Henry had asked him to help him move a load of logs on a hand-cart, ready for the winter.

Spencer knocked on the door and after a few moments, Henry cautiously opened it. On seeing Spencer, Henry beamed and invited him in. It seemed colder inside than it had been walking the few miles to the cottage.

Henry shuffled across the room and leant heavily on the kitchen table as he lowered himself back onto his chair. The cottage consisted of just one room. A small range provided heat and a place to cook. Iron pans were hung alongside on the chimney breast. Apart from the table and chairs there was little furniture. An old-fashioned wooden settle was placed near the range with a rug draped over its back and a well-worn cushion nestled in one corner. Towards the rear Spencer could make out a bed, half-concealed by a curtain across the room.

Henry invited Spencer to sit in the other chair at the table. Before long the conversation turned to the crops, or lack of them.

"I'm pleased you've come. I've been wondering how to get the news to you. I've decided to pack it all in."

This was not news that Spencer had wanted to hear, but not totally unexpected. Years of hard manual work, out in all weathers had taken its toll. Although hale and hearty in many ways, rheumatism and arthritis had badly affected his hands which were disfigured and stiff, and his hips and back were perpetually painful.

"Landlord wants me out," Henry explained. "Wants the land for houses. More money in it. I'm to go by Lady Day."

Spencer did a quick calculation – that was only about eight weeks away. His heart sank once more.

"I'm going back to Essendon. I'll live with my nephew and his wife. 'Tis the only family I have left now. Don't 'spect she's that happy about it, but there you are. What's to be done? I don't think I'll trouble them for long. Well past my 'three-score years and ten'."

Spencer could see tears welling in Henry's eyes as he contemplated his new life and tried to make the best of it.

"Now, you're afeared of what's to become of you. Don't you worry on that score. I have a friend, well an acquaintance, really," Henry pronounced the word very deliberately, "He's head gardener at Yoakley's, not two miles from here. They need an under-gardener and I've put you forward for the job. There's good work there. Kitchen garden like you're used to and parkland and fancy gardens, an' all. You'll suit, I've told him so! Anyway, you get yourself over there as soon as you may and talk to Mr Jordan."

Spencer was more than a little taken aback. His mind raced with questions and objections but he was completely lost for words.

"Oh, an' if you're wond'ring about lodgings, there's a cottage comes with the job. They like to keep you handy these rich types!"

Spencer glanced out of the window. The sky was darkening again. He hoped it would be rain rather than more snow, but the grey light promised the latter and he thought it would be wise to start for home. As he left, he took Henry firmly by his crumpled hand and wished him well for his new life with his nephew. He realised he may never see him again.

The walk home gave Spencer plenty of time to think. Effectively he had no job, no income. If he took the step and found this Mr Jordan, he might have both. Lizzie wouldn't like it though. She hated change. But perhaps she could get work in the 'big house' too. Primrose would have to change schools, but that shouldn't be an obstacle. He reckoned he had nothing to lose by trying. The hard part would be convincing Lizzie. Then he remembered Robert.

Cooper called a meeting of his senior staff to discuss the future of the company, and he was his usual positive self.

"The omnibus trade is popular, and despite competition from other providers we are still making good profits. The long-distance services are running on a tight budget, partly through excessive toll charges, but we can still supply a service cheaper than the horse carriage. However, the trials in Lancashire *are* more troubling. The fad for putting carriages on rails seems to be taking off. Stephenson's machine is gaining favour, and advances in the system are developing fast. Rainhill has inspired an interest in railway locomotives and I am afraid it will draw investors away from road steam transport and towards rail steam transport."

"It makes no sense," Walter declared, "The outlay for building tracks and locomotives far outweighs that for building steam carriages. We, all of us at the forefront of road team transport, have had so few accidents with our machines but that, and the tragic events at the trials are overlooked. It seems the fashion is for rail – and the inventors have persuasive, if misguided, champions for their enterprise."

Robert agreed. He had also heard of the popularity of the idea of transport on rails. "But surely it is unlikely to evolve into serious competition. After all steam carriages use roads that already exist, whereas railroads need to be built at great expense. Steam carriages can ascend and descend hills with supreme ease, while the rail machines can only tackle level roads or small inclines at best!"

Cooper revealed that Parliament was going to investigate the question of excessive tolls and false reports of road damage, steam carriages alarming horses, and dangerously exploding. "I, myself, have been called to give evidence," he preened ever so slightly, "along with other eminent gentlemen; Colonel Torrens, Mr Gurney and Mr Hancock have also been called."

******

Robert returned home that evening, later than usual. The house was quiet, Primrose and William were in bed, and Lizzie, busy in the scullery, hadn't heard him come through the door. He went to the scullery and, meaning to call out to Lizzie, leaned against the door jamb. He watched as she plunged her hands into the water in the sink, absorbed by whatever chore she was about. A wayward straggle of hair fell across her cheek and she absent-mindedly pushed it back behind her ear.

"Always working," Robert thought. No matter what time of day, Lizzie always seemed to have chores to do. William's birth had not been easy and he continued to be a demanding child. He'd still wake a dozen times a night, it seemed to Robert, who would be woken by his cries until his mother rocked and comforted him. Spencer and Primrose slept on unaware. Spencer in a deep sleep and Primrose woken but soon asleep again, in the sure knowledge that her baby brother was safely in his mother's arms. He was nearly three now, and despite Lizzie's best efforts with pap and "a li'l drop o' gin" sleepless nights were still to be expected.

A wave of compassion cascaded through Robert's body. He was taken aback by the feeling and involuntarily made a sound. Lizzie turned, surprised to see him.

"Oh, 'allo Robert. I didn't 'ear you come in."

"Uh," Robert cleared his throat, "I was just wondering if Spencer was at home."

"Oh, no, 'e's gone to see someone … 'bout somefing. Thought 'e'd be back by now. Pot's cold, but I can 'eat y' somefing if y' want t' eat."

Robert thought she looked worried, but sensed it wasn't because Spencer was late home.

"No, no, don't worry. I'm sure you've had enough of chores for today."

Lizzie smiled at him, grateful for not having to come away from her task. At that moment Spencer noisily opened the front door.

"Sorry, I'm back so late," he called loudly to Lizzie.

"Ssh," she returned, "You'll wake the littl'uns."

"Oh, yeah. Ssshh, ssshh." he staggered a little as he came in. "Went to see ol' Elkins on me way back. Told 'im the good news and we 'ad a tot or two of brandy. 'E's alright, is Elkins. Good bloke. 'E's proper choked that 'e's gotta get out." He caught sight of Robert in the shadows. "Oh, sorry Lizzie!" Spencer rubbed the side of his nose and gave a lopsided wink, to indicate he knew something but wasn't letting on. "'Allo Robert. What you doin' 'ere?"

It seemed a silly question as he lived there, but it was obvious Spencer had had more than a bit too much to drink.

"I think I will retire early tonight. It has been a busy day."

"Ho, yus! I think that maybe I shall retire early has well." Spencer spoke deliberately, with an affected accent and staggered a little closer to Lizzie.

Robert went up to his room. He realised he was actually quite hungry and would have welcomed a dishful of whatever was in the cooking pot, but he knew he couldn't stay downstairs. He'd never seen Spencer so drunk before. Whatever he'd been doing, he'd find out in due course.

As he lay in bed, he reflected on that moment a few minutes earlier. He felt confused and conflicted. Spencer and Lizzie had been good to him since the day he arrived on their doorstep; good landlords and they had become good friends. Primrose had grown up with him always there. He doubted she could remember a time when he wasn't. She was growing fast and was doing well at school. He sometimes brought home scraps of paper from his work and had bought her a dipping pen and ink so she could practise her letters. Spencer and Robert enjoyed growing a few vegetables in the back yard and Robert had taught him how to fish in the nearby River Lea. But perhaps the time had come when he should find somewhere new to live. And without him to wash and cook for, Lizzie would have a little less to do. With the vision of Lizzie tucking back that strand of hair, and his mind firing off thoughts that never reached a conclusion, he eventually fell asleep.

******

John Cooper returned to his own, far more luxurious, home and fired with enthusiasm and visions of the future, he once again wrote to his friend and confidant…

... I was concerned. In the early days it looked like my great adventure was going to fail. There was such opposition to steam transport. I particularly remember reading

about an 'explosive engine' – what a fearful name! – instead of steam providing the power, force was to be generated by exploding a gas inside a small cylinder inside the engine. It was designed to force a piston along the cylinder and connecting rods could then power machinery, thus making the need for steam and furnaces redundant. Experimental engines of the type had been built – but I'm glad to say it came to nothing.

But then we had a great good fortune, although perhaps I should not call it so. When the late King died, there was a great clamour to see the Royal Body lying in state in Windsor. Well, of course, we were in an ideal position!

I arranged rooms at an inn in the town and soon had bookings for several expeditions to Windsor. All manner of people wished to show their respects (and to be seen to be doing so) even if their opinion of the King had been less than favourable during his lifetime. Their reasons were of no concern of ours, but their custom was a great boon to my company, and it helped to establish our venture as a regular way to travel...

After several more pages extoling his great accomplishments, he concluded:

.... It is with all modesty, I must confide that I am shortly to be summoned to Parliament. They wish to call upon my extensive knowledge of the steam carriage business. Not me alone of, course. Some others whose names I'm sure will be familiar to you. Colonel T_____, Mr G_____ (a man with extraordinary inventive talents) and Mr H_____, to name but three.

(I'm afraid I cannot name them in full, for reasons of confidentiality!) I am certain that after we have set the record straight, a secure future for steam carriages (and my own business) will be assured.

    With my deepest
    regards to yourself and your
    dear wife,
        Yours, ever truly,
        John C.

15

1834

Spencer's news had come as a complete surprise; it was the last thing Robert had expected. Still, he understood why Spencer must make the move to Stoke Newington, and wished them all well. He had had time to look for a new place to live and found a small apartment nearer to the centre of Hackney. He had two rooms above a cobbler's; small and no garden. Not permanent, he told himself, but good enough for now. He took to having his meals in the nearby King's Head and arranged for a washerwoman to do his laundry and the 'odd bit of cleaning'.

The King's Head looked like it had been there for ever. It was a small, irregular-shaped building with low ceilings and uneven floors. There was a tall bow window to the left of the door and a low multi-paned window to the right. As you stepped down into the front bar you were welcomed by the smell of old tobacco and centuries of ale. The room was furnished with half a dozen wooden tables and chairs. A fire burned in the grate to the right, where a couple of tall barrel-like chairs sat ready for customers to warm themselves. Only one was ever occupied.

The ale-house was run by Chas and Martha, Ma to the 'regulars'. Their son, Ben, worked as a potboy and they employed a young woman, Louise, as a servant and to work in the bar rooms. As the weeks passed, Robert began to recognise the regulars. He nodded a greeting to a pair of older men who passed the evening by playing cribbage, and to a couple who routinely sat by the bay window. She always wore a hat that once had borne a bright display of artificial flowers but now looked a little forlorn, and he wore the coat of a labourer. The man occupying the chair by the fire had a shabby blue-grey greatcoat that looked as if it had been made for a much bigger man. He never spoke to anyone but would stare into the fire, mumbling softly to himself, and sometimes shouting abruptly out loud. Robert wondered what pictures he saw in the flames, that kept him so occupied.

Robert had adopted a seat with a table. With his back to the wall and a good view of the comings and goings through the door, he spent most evenings reading the latest edition of his favourite satirical journal. Louise approached his table, smiling, "What's it to be tonight? The pie as usual?"

"No, I think I'll have a change tonight. Do you have any turbot?"

"Fresh in today."

"That'll be grand, thank you Louise." Robert returned to his reading until his meal arrived.

"Would you like another drink…?" Louise indicated his empty tankard as she put the dish on the table. "You know, you've been coming in for months now and I still don't know your name."

"Robert," Robert replied.

"Ah Robbie! Are you Scotch?"

Robert had never been called Robbie before and smiled. "No, Westmorland – the north of England. And, yes, thank you."

"See, I guessed you're not from round here."

Robert was fascinated by Louise. She had wild black curly hair that she tried to keep tamed by tying it back with a ribbon, and a dark exotic complexion. Her eyes were wide and bright and her manner treated every customer as a long-held friend, inducing every one to be disposed to return to the ale-house. After this short exchange he found himself reading less of his journals and spending more time just watching her as she went about her work.

Gradually they got to know a little more about each other until Robert eventually found the courage to ask her if she would like to accompany him to the theatre in Stepney.

Their outings became a regular occurrence, that Robert increasingly looked forward to. He told Louise about why he had come to London, and how he was now practically estranged from his older brother. Louise was reluctant to say much about her past, other than she was the daughter of a ship's captain. He hoped she would feel able to explain more in time. On one of their omnibus journeys back to Hackney, their hands had touched, and slipped unconsciously into one another. When he left her at her lodgings, he kissed her gently on the cheek. He thought about that kiss all the way home.

The bond between them grew and strengthened. They shared and understood the difficulties and disappointments they had endured in their younger lives and delighted in the moments of joy each had found in seemingly insignificant events such as the sound of a brook or the colours of autumn. She made him laugh and he made her feel he recognised she was more than 'just a serving girl'. They found they had much in common, from a love of poetry and reading, to a strong desire for social reform and a frustration at their inadequacy to make any difference. Sometimes they would talk long into the night, putting the world to rights and enjoying each other's company.

******

Robert kept in touch with Spencer, through letters and the occasional 'family pic-nic' when they could all get together. Having had a late start, Spencer's reading and writing had progressed dramatically. He had a good neat hand and enjoyed writing to Robert about the methods and devices that the gardeners used. Primrose would often add a little note of her own, and illustrate it with small sketch.

Spencer's duties were mainly in the kitchen garden. They had a glasshouse and even an orangery, so he had got his wish, and was perfecting how to grow cucumbers. Lizzie had work in the linen room in the manor and was content with her new life. Primrose had settled in a new school and William joined when he was old enough. The children had made friends with two other children whose parents worked on the estate and went to the same school. They were allowed to play on the drying green as it was out of sight of any windows of the manor house. But it was difficult to play quietly so occasionally they would slip off into the surrounding parkland and climb trees or make dens. When their parents found out, they were under strict instructions 'not to be seen or heard' but they had keen eyes and ears and would soon make themselves invisible if they heard a horse or carriage approaching. On one occasion they almost stumbled into two ladies from the house taking a stroll in a wooded part of the estate. Luckily a fallen beech tree was close-by and they squeezed between it and the ground and held their breath hoping the ladies would not choose to rest against it. They couldn't believe how slowly two people could walk. William kept peeping out to see how far they had gone and was frantically signalled back by his sister who could still hear the murmur of their conversation. After what seemed like hours, but was probably no more than fifteen minutes, the children emerged from their hiding place, smeared with mud and with a light coating of leaves and beech mast. They brushed it off as best they could, but were sure they were in for a telling off when they got home.

**** 16 ****

1837

Just when Robert felt his life was settled and comfortable, circumstances determined otherwise. Walter was looking concerned when Robert arrived for work.

"Cooper's called a meeting. Ten o'clock. I think we can guess what's coming."

"We are in a time of change," Cooper pronounced to his senior staff. "Change is all around us but the stubborn heads of so many are not ready to embrace it. Change brings uncertainty. We have a new queen, who is no more than a child, and who knows where she will lead us! I do not mean to be disrespectful," he quickly added, "but I fear the old guard in parliament will take control because they will not wish to let someone so unfamiliar with politics and commerce interfere with the daily business of the nation. We have been fighting for years to get the road tolls reduced and the Parliamentary Committee, of which I was a participant, you may remember, has stated the case plainly. We were effective. A Bill was passed in the Commons. But the Lords, in their wisdom, have rejected it. We have achieved nothing. We have shown over and over again that steam carriages are not only a viable means of transport, but safe, efficient and comfortable. We have run several excursions to Brighton, being able to complete the return journey in little more than twelve hours – and with no major mishaps. We have carried eminent engineers and other worthy folk, all of whom have reported in our favour. We have shown steam carriages do not harm the roads, and the services can be run without the huge expense and disruption of building flat swathes of railroad across the country. But we have been met with nothing but prejudice, ignorance and, yes, I will say it, wilful opposition."

Cooper paused. His staff were well aware of the situation. "And so, I have made a difficult decision."

The men looked on, what was he going to announce?

"I have decided to sell the business."

A small gasp filled the silence.

"I am in negotiations to purchase a modest property in Hampshire. It is delightfully situated, with a trout stream running through the estate and some of the most upstanding families of the county live close by." Cooper realised he was deviating from the matter the men wished to know most. "The company will continue, but I do not know what direction the new owner will wish to take. Regretfully, there certainly will not be an opportunity for more innovation with steam vehicles. Except for one last task I ask of you. It will be some months before all the matters are settled, and in that time, I should like you to adapt our carriages to devise a small vehicle for my personal use. It will need a pilot of course, which I intend to be myself, and an engineer who can also stoke the furnace. Beyond that I wish it to have comfortable seating for four, or no more than six guests. It will be my joy to traverse the country roads and show the populace what an invention they have spurned!

"Now I have delayed you from your work, long enough. I need you to complete the tasks on which you are currently employed. There will be no long-distance services beyond those already contracted. Maintenance of our fleet must be upheld until the business is sold and our city services also cease. I look forward to seeing your plans for my new vehicle. I'm sure you will have contrived a plan by the end of the week. Oh, and meanwhile, not a word to the other employees!"

With that, the men were dismissed from Cooper's office and he set about inventing a name for his new machine He doodled a monogram on some headed letter paper.

As soon as they were out of earshot the men broke into discussion. Some were concerned for their futures, and their families. Some were concerned for the labourers, although there was comfort in knowing the firm would continue in some form. And some were inspired to adapt their designs for Cooper's latest notion: a miniature carriage for personal use.

Robert surmised that the new owners would make money-saving changes, including dismissing some of the senior staff. He discussed the problem with Louise.

"I think I should look for employment in another company. One that's working with steam engines. I've got somewhere in mind. I've worked with them on some of Cooper's proving trips."

"Who are you thinking of?" Louise asked. "Are they close by? Will you still live here?"

"No, they're south of the river. So not far away. But it'll mean moving lodgings, I think."

"If that is what you want, then you must do it." Louise seemed a little unhappy at the plan, but said nothing.

******

A few days later, Robert got his opportunity. A machine had broken one of its cutting tools and someone needed to go to the supplier for a replacement. Robert volunteered to go, saying he was a bit slack of work in the workshop. The journey took him south of the river and as he crossed the Thames on the new London Bridge, he recalled the trip he had made with Spencer. It was strange to think the old bridge, that had served for so many years, had gone and soon there would be no trace of it left. This time, instead of turning left to the tunnel entrance (where work was underway once again), his route took him westward towards Westminster Bridge and a higgledy-piggledy group of buildings, behind which was a cacophony of industry and invention.

Robert was taken to the appropriate part of the works and explained what was required. It was going to take a little while to make the new cutter but he could have it today if he was prepared to wait. He thought that was a better option than having to return another day.

"Is Mr Field on the premises?" he asked. "I should like to speak with him."

The clerk led Robert around the works to Mr Field's office.

"A Mr Houghton to see you, sir." The clerk enquired if Field was free for an unexpected visitor. Field looked up from the papers on his desk, his face showing he was still engaged with whatever he had just been considering.

"Houghton? Ah, yes, young Mr Houghton. Come in, my dear fellow, come in."

Robert gave a brief explanation of why he had come to the works.

"Mm, steam carriages. We've concluded they are not a line we want to continue. Machine tools, standardising working parts that's the future. Well, that's our small-side. Much of our energy is spent on steam engines for ships. In fact, we are waiting for SS Great Western to arrive any day. She's sailing from Bristol and we'll fit her out with two magnificent engines for her paddle wheels."

"Yes, I heard she had launched successfully. And there's plans to sail her to New York?"

"The fastest, and most luxurious, passenger steam ship in the world – if our engines perform as we predict."

"No locomotive engines?"

"No, it's not a manufactory we're competing in, although we've been able to demonstrate some improvements to designs. Too much competition in the midlands and the north to make it worthwhile. And anyway, we have access to the most important river and sea routes – so ships make more sense."

"It seems locomotives are here to stay," Robert acknowledged. "The line to Greenwich is taking shape. I glimpsed the railway as I crossed London Bridge. I would have thought building a railway without the intention of carrying freight to be a risky venture. Surely there cannot be enough people who want to travel that way to make it worthwhile. Do you think it will be a success?"

"It seems it is a great success already. And completion of the line with a terminus by the river has made it more so. Thousands of passengers each day use it to get to the city. And I must admit when the line is extended to Greenwich it will be a benefit to us – as we are often in discussions with the Admiralty and have to make journeys to the naval dockyards. When you have time, I would encourage you to explore the line a little. It is the most ingenious idea. Three or four miles of solid brick viaduct – so there is no gradient and no disruption to road or rail traffic where it crosses the roads. Further to that, some of the arches of the viaduct are faced and let out for trade or storage. Income from the line and from below – clever!"

"I shall never be convinced," Robert continued. "You hear of nothing but dreadful accidents on these routes. It is the mothers of the children I feel most sympathy for."

"It is true, there have been far too many fatalities on the railways. But they are not always the fault of the line owners. Some people seem unable to grasp what a powerful machine a railway locomotive and its train of carriages is. And of course, a fence is a challenge to a small boy. Especially if he is bolstered by the egging-on of his companions. Small boys and railway engines seem to have an inexplicable attraction. I suppose it is the novelty. I'm sure it will pass in time."

The conversation lapsed and Robert thought he had best come to the point before Field indicated it was time to leave. He explained the situation at Cooper's and wondered if there would be an opening for him here.

Field promised he would discuss the proposition with the other directors and let him know their decision. Robert left the office with a faint notion of hope.

17

March 1838

Within a few months it had all been settled. Cooper had moved in to his new country home and had his 'Cooper's Compact Conveyance', tastefully decorated with an insignia made from three Cs. Looking not unlike the emblem for the Isle of Man, it embellished the front of the vehicle and formed the terminal to each of the axle ends. He had been invited to many soirees and dinner parties by his new neighbours, but whether it was Cooper's engaging personality, or the novelty of his new carriage that had prompted the invitations, it was hard to tell.

The new owners of his company had dropped steam carriages from their enterprise and the employees engaged in the daily omnibus services had had to find new work. Many had chosen to join the growing numbers of horse-drawn omnibus companies and some had found work as drivers or firemen on the railways. The senior staff had been retained, for the time being at least, as they knew the business and had the connections with suppliers and clients.

Robert was pleased to have found a new position with *Maudslay, Son and Field*'s engineering company but his heart was broken when the decision to leave Cooper's was finally made. When he had discussed the situation with Louise, she had encouraged him at every step. He had assumed she would come with him across the river but she explained she could not leave the life she had made for herself in Hackney.

After working for some years at the King's Head, she had received a legacy from her father. She had used it to set up a small school-room for the poorer children close-by. She had encouraged the local shop-keepers to pay a subscription to help with funding, declaring that by keeping the children occupied they would have less time to get up to mischief by breaking windows or pilfering their stock. The children only paid what their parents could afford – in some cases nothing at all – but she felt she was doing some good by teaching the children the rudiments of reading and writing.

"Why do you make your engines, Robbie?" Robert had never thought about 'why' before. "Is it to benefit the human race or the challenge of the new science? Perhaps those coachmen and stable-boys and farmers are right to be concerned for their livelihoods.

"You go and make your splendid engines that will change the way we travel. I want to stay here and use my small engine of education to try to make a difference to how the ordinary person is treated.

"I'm accepted here," she explained, "daughter of an English sea captain and an African bought from a Maryland slave owner. There's not so many like me, and although they may not say it aloud, some people don't like to see us together. It would be as hard for you as it would be for me."

She said they had shared some wonderful moments but it was time for him to start a new life. He implored her to come but she was adamant.

Robert found new lodgings in Lambeth not far from the river. His landlady, Mrs Perkins, was a middle-aged lady, who, after becoming a widow, kept a lodging house for 'respectable gentlemen'.

There were three other boarders, as well as Robert. One was a printer, another a solicitor's clerk and the third made scientific instruments.

Robert didn't get to see Louise or Spencer and the family so often, but kept up his correspondence with them all and enjoyed following their progress. He missed Louise terribly. She was, he thought, a wonderful, vital person – never quick to judge and always ready to accept people, trying to understand how life's obstacles had made them what they were. But the vitality that made her strong also made her single-minded. No matter what had passed between them, her school was her life now, and there was no room for him.

Many times, he wondered if he had been too eager to 'jump ship' from Cooper's works – he might have been able to keep a senior position there, but it was done now. He rose early for his first day at work. Robert's new employers were very well thought of for the manufacture of steam engines for ships, and Robert had to quickly learn the intricacies of their design.

"This is Mr Lambert. He's one of our valued engineers. And this is Mr Houghton." Field introduced the two men and they nodded to each other in acknowledgement.

"And this is Mr Thomas. You'll be working together."

"Arthur," the other man said, and held out his hand.

"Robert," Robert replied, shaking his hand.

Both men looked younger than Robert but obviously well-regarded by their employers.

After some discussions, Lambert returned to his work while Arthur took Robert on a quick tour of the works.

"This is our Small Shed," he said as they entered a huge workshop. "It's where we make the small stuff, machine parts and so on."

He led Robert through to another huge building. "Here we're making the parts for the marine engines, and over there are the rigs for the stationary engines and locomotives."

Both sheds were filled with the sounds of hammering and lathes turning. Dozens of men skilful with their tools and busy at their tasks. In some places, men were shouting and calling and there was the clank and burr of chains lifting parts into position as engines were assembled or part-assembled, ready to be moved on to the company's clients. As they talked, Robert detected Arthur's northern accent, but guessed he was from the other side of the Pennines.

"Ol' Lambert's not from round here either," Arthur explained. "Almost Scottish, he is. Guess we've all come south following the work. One of my brothers, Alfred, he's here too – he's in the Small Shed."

Robert thought his own reason for coming south wasn't entirely due to finding work, but said nothing.

******

Working on a much larger scale than he had been used to, Robert's first few weeks were daunting.

"It's like working with magnificent, powerful dray-horses after being used to the elegant, compact ponies of the steam carriages," Robert explained to Spencer. "They both work in fundamentally the same way but you have to treat them differently and respect their particularities."

However, his work must have been valued as he was soon appointed to the team that was installing the engines in *SS Great Western*.

"It's strange," Robert confided to Arthur one day, "to be working on a project of the young Mr Brunel. I first heard of him from a very shady character, mmm, fourteen, fifteen years ago. Then I was able to visit his tunnel under the Thames – before that dreadful accident when so many lives were lost and the project halted. Brunel had a lucky escape that day, I think. And imagine, if he had not been heard by his rescuers, we would not be here working on this ship today! I never pictured he would be so prominent in my life."

"Well, we'll never sail on a ship like this. This is for the gentry. But I think his railways will affect everyone's lives. Mr Brunel will be significant to us all, one way or another. And tomorrow you may get to see your hero!"

******

It was an exciting and nerve-wracking day for all involved. The first voyage of the impressive ship had to go without any snags. Reputations were relying on it. The two huge engines to drive the paddle wheels had been fitted, adapted and, hopefully, perfected. The furnaces were fired and stoked until they brought the system ready for steaming and, when the tide was right, the orders were given to cast off.

Robert and his fellow engineers were grouped in the engine-room, checking gauges, watching for leaking joints and monitoring the smooth running of the pistons. The stokers kept at their task and everything was progressing perfectly. The log-line had shown she had reached a speed of some fifteen knots. The senior engineer went up to the saloon to report to Mr Brunel where he was being detained by the dignitaries on board. Although they were not much further than Tilbury, and not yet in the open sea, Robert was still not used to the motion on-board a ship, nor the smells of the oil and the furnace in the confined space of the engine-room. He could feel his stomach turning over and the saliva building in his mouth. All seemed well, there were others there to attend to any problems, and he was sure he would feel better if he went up to the deck for a while.

He held the handrail firmly, connecting with the cool brass, still damp from the morning dew and concentrated on watching the buildings on the distant horizon. The height of the ship gave him a good view over the flat land of the estuary, and although he couldn't name them, he noted the church towers and steeples in the distance. That, and the rhythmic stamping of the paddle-wheels as they cut through the water, helped to turn his thoughts away from his churning stomach. Suddenly his attention was brought back to the ship.

"Fire! Fire!" someone yelled.

He turned to see smoke billowing from the deck, close to the funnel.

Panic and helplessness held him still, then propelled him down the shaft ladder back to the engine-room. It was black with smoke, men were choking and running with buckets. He covered his face with his arm and went closer to the engines to see what was amiss. Meanwhile, others in the crew, assembled with military precision and set the water-pumping engine into action. Another went straight to the stern of the ship to eject a barrel of gunpowder that was being stored in the lazaretto. The commotion reached the ears of Mr Brunel who was seen hurtling towards the ladder that Robert had descended a few minutes before. In his haste, he missed his footing and fell heavily to the floor twenty feet below.

The newspapers in the following days gave the event a lot of publicity, but perhaps not exactly what the directors of the owning company would have liked.

Despite it being very early in the morning, a crowd had gathered to watch the event, and on seeing the ship ease into the river, cheers could be heard by the company on board, and was no doubt gratifying to Mr Brunel (jnr) and his eminent companions who were overseeing the proceedings. The engines and paddle wheels performed well and in little over an hour they were already reaching Sheerness. Then the alarm was raised. Smoke had been spotted bellowing from the deck close to the funnel. Further investigation showed the root of the fire was in the engine room, which was now thick with suffocating smoke and hampered attempts to slow the engines.

There was also great concern that a quantity of gunpowder on board the ship might be caught in the conflagration and cause unimaginable damage. It seemed S. S. Great Western's maiden voyage under steam might be her last and she was run onto the shore to allow the passengers and crew not involved in the fire-fighting to evacuate the ship.

Portable engines and water pumps which had been installed for just such an emergency were brought into action and the men battled against the fire for more than two hours. The flames could be seen a good way off and caught the attention of the crew of the *Pearl* which hove to, to give what assistance they could.

Although the fire was dramatic and at first looked life-threatening, it was eventually discovered to be confined to a small area of the engine room and caused when felt lagging to the boilers had ignited due to an error in its application.

We can confirm that three of the company were injured during the unfortunate incident but are now safely on-board the hospital-ship *Dreadnought* at Greenwich.

The following day, more dramatic news emerged:

Following the catastrophic fire on board S. S. Great Western on Saturday, we have received further distressing intelligence.

Mr Brunel, being on-board his record-breaking vessel, was called for to give advice and assistance in the calamity. In the confusion of the emergency he fell some forty feet from the deck to the engine room. On being lifted from the bowels of the ship he was found to be most-dreadfully injured. With all possible speed he was conveyed to Holyhaven on the northern shore of the river, where he was attended by a surgeon. The health of the young and prodigious engineer is in a precarious state, where he is believed to have sustained a dislocated shoulder and a broken leg.

Rumours of the accident soon became a matter of interest and excitement.

"Was he very badly hurt?" a colleague eagerly enquired of Robert. "Will he survive this accident? What about the ship? It doesn't sound good."

Robert felt a duty to the ship's owners and Mr Brunel himself to try to lessen the damage the over-zealous reporting of the accident would do to the ship.

"It was a bad fall, but he is recovering well. The ship suffered only minimal damage. A lot of the smoke was from the extinguishing of the wet felt – like burning wet leaves, a lot of smoke but no heat! It was all quickly repaired and in all the voyage to Bristol was only delayed by four hours. I'm told

Great Western's breadth of beam makes her a very stable vessel but I do not envy those seeking to reach America in her!

"There was great excitement at the ship's arrival in Bristol. I have heard thousands of people are taking advantage of visiting her to see the splendid furnishings before her voyage to New York next week."

"He must feel the gods are against him, what with the Tunnel getting flooded again."

"Yes, it's not been the best of times for him. But I'm sure we will hear more of his ideas in the future."

18

June 1838

"Are y' going to the coronation?" Lizzie asked Robert. The 'family' group were enjoying an afternoon in London Fields and Robert was trying to understand the intricacies of the rules of cricket.

"Well, I haven't had my invitation yet."

"No, y' silly 'apeth," Lizzie chuckled, "I mean, are y' going to watch the pr'cession?"

"No, I don't think I will, it's not something that interests me, and seems to be an awful waste of money."

"Aww, we are, ain't we, love?" Lizzie turned to Spencer.

"Well, the missus 'as told us we are not to miss seeing the young queen. Would break 'er 'eart if we didn't go."

"They say she's just like a little doll, an' beau'iful too. You want to see 'er too, don't y' Primrose." Primrose nodded dutifully.

"Will she be wearing 'er crown?" William asked, "An' is it *real* gold?"

"Well, for part of the day. But it's too heavy to wear all the time." Primrose completed a daisy chain she was making and twirled it onto William's head. "Your majesty," she said solemnly, and bowed deeply.

"Stop it! Daisy chains is for girls. I'm not a girl!" and he snatched it off at threw it at his sister.

Primrose just smiled and put it on her own head instead.

"You should go, Robert," Lizzie continued. "I'm sure you'll be sorry if y' don't. It's an 'oliday y' know. We're goin' to get there early, ain't we?"

Spencer looked resignedly at Robert.

Robert turned to Primrose. "How's work in the Big House?" Since leaving school, Primrose had managed to get work alongside her mother.

"I'm in the kitchens now. I like it better there. I try to remember how everything's prepared and cooked an' I write it all down when I get 'ome."

"She's got a proper big book wiv it all in," her mother interrupted. "She even draws little pictures of 'ow it's put on the dishes. Work of art, it is."

"That sounds very diligent, Primrose. And an excellent idea if you want to run your own kitchen one day."

"Not just the kitchen, I want to be a housekeeper, like Mrs Dale. I'm good wiv figures an' I could keep the books as well as she does. But for now, I'm in the scullery for the most part."

"What about you, William? Are you doing well at school?"

"It's alright. But I like it best when I can go out with Pa and help in the woods. We got a big ol' bough off an oak tree the other week, didn't we Pa? You should 'ave 'eard it when it came down. Made the ground shake it was so big!"

"The bough was dead, 'ad to come off. Tell 'im abaht y' primroses though."

"Oh, well, they 'ad some primroses what was purple instead of the proper yellow, see. 'An I fought, 'What would 'appen if the yellow ones an' the purple ones got mixed up?' So Pa let me 'ave a little spot in the glasshouse an' I got the pollen from one an' put it on flower of the other – to get some seeds, see."

"And what did happen?" Robert was intrigued.

"Well, we don't know yet. But they did make seeds. We've just gotta wait and see what grows. If anyfing. Pa says they might not make plants."

"Well, let me know if they do. Purple and yellow primroses would be a real novelty."

******

Lizzie was up first on Coronation Day. Her excitement at the thought of seeing the Queen was mixed with anxiety about getting her own arrangements in order. She packed a basket with cheese and bread and water because "They'll all be on the make and charge wicked prices for food." She also put a small pot in the basket.

"It's alright for you and William," she explained to Spencer. "You can go an' find an alley and stand against the wall. But Primmy and me can't do that. This way we can hold the pot under our skirts and empty it later – somewhere." she added vaguely.

"This is madness!" Spencer looked out of the window at the rain pouring down.

"It'll stop soon. You see if it don't. Rain before seven…" She didn't complete the saying. Spencer was well aware of its optimism. "It's just a summer shower."

Lizzie produced some lengths of oil-cloth to keep the worst of the rain off herself and her three reluctant companions and they set off in their summer Sunday Best on the four-mile walk to the centre of the city.

Spencer had calculated that somewhere near Charing Cross would be a good vantage point to see the procession. The rain eased as they got nearer to their destination and they noticed more and more people were also heading in the same direction.

"Ooh look," Lizzie pointed, "That building's got flags out!"

"And that one," William added. "And that one. And that one's got a star and a big VR, see!"

Soon there were so many decorations to notice, it was no longer a novelty. Lizzie just grinned at the sights. They reached Trafalgar Square shortly after half past seven.

"We'll be there far too early," Spencer had complained. But on seeing the crowds already gathering, he reluctantly agreed their early start had not been ill-judged. "We'd best get a spot before we're too late."

All the space close to the route was already filled and they settled on a place outside the new National Gallery. Its elevated position would give them a reasonable view but Lizzie was disappointed she could not be closer. Everywhere it was possible, platforms, some rickety and some more substantial, had been built to give the spectators a better view; even the statue of Charles the First was covered and made available for seating. On either side of the statue was a group of soldiers in red tunics and gleaming silver helmets.

"Can't we go down there?" Lizzie pointed to a half-occupied trestle table.

"Yer better off 'ere, lady," the gentleman next to Lizzie advised. "They're charging ten shillin's or more to stand in them places, and they're probably already taken anyway."

"Ten shillings! to stand on a table?" Lizzie didn't believe him.

"Oh yeah, and even more if y' want a seat in those posh 'ouses."

As they stood and defended their little bit of territory they had a chance to take in all the decorations the homes and businesses had contrived. It was easy to tell where the monied people lived because their decorations were more extravagant and grand. Every window was filled with people or with chairs waiting for their occupants. "Look, there's even people on the roofs!" Primrose exclaimed. "How did they get up there?"

"Will it be starting soon?" William asked.

"No, we've still got a bit of a wait." Spencer looked towards the black cloud that was approaching and guessed they were in for another soaking. William, tired of the view, sat amongst the legs and feet of the adults around him and produced four painted wooden soldiers from his jacket, who commenced to fight a determined battle.

As Spencer had feared, the rain began to fall again. Within seconds umbrellas appeared form nowhere and covered the scene in front of them with a mosaic, resembling an artistic tiled floor. The shower passed quickly and the crowd soon regained its optimistic good humour. The early-morning sunshine and the residue of the rain gave an extra sparkle to the scene. Occasionally, one of the make-shift stands would collapse, to the great amusement of those not involved. Luckily no serious injuries seemed to be sustained and the edifices were soon rebuilt and reoccupied. Singing would spontaneously be heard from small groups and the song would spread through the crowd, everyone now an ally in the battle against any newly-arriving invaders. Traders mingled through the crowd offering keepsakes of the occasion. Lizzie urged Spencer to buy some flags, but hearing they were sixpence each reduced her purchase to two, instead of four.

"Keep your money close," she whispered to Spencer. "There's bound to be dippers abaht."

She waved her flag happily, watching the route for any sign of the event commencing. "Look, William, look!" she pointed to the line of the road where soldiers and policemen were beginning to take their stations to form a human barrier against the crowd. "Don't they look smart in their uniforms?"

Now and again a black carriage would make its way down Whitehall. "Is that the procession?" Primrose asked, getting bored and tired of waiting.

"No, that'll be someone who's invited to the ceremony in the abbey. I dunno who though. Politician prob'ly."

Suddenly a noise like thunder came from the distance. Lizzie jumped and William stood up, eager to see what was happening.

"That'll be the cannon to signal the start. It'll be a while before they get here though."

A great cheer echoed through the crowd and a nearby church bell rang out in celebration. At almost the same time some trumpeters and drummers who had been with the soldiers near Charles's statue moved into position closer to the road. This forced the crowd who had occupied that spot to find new accommodation, which in turn meant poaching on someone else's ground. A slight scuffle broke out on the western side of the road as the occupants defended their line. Soldiers drew their swords and policemen brandished their truncheons. Spencer's heart quickened as he recalled the 'trouble' there had been several years before at the funeral procession of the late Queen Caroline, when two onlookers were killed when firearms had been used to calm the crowd. This time though, the incident passed without further problems and somehow, room was made for all.

Eventually, a military band could be heard approaching and ahead of them the first of the procession and carriages. Cheers went up as they came in to view and flags were eagerly waved.

Then came an assembly of men in bright red uniforms walking before the first of the carriages, each drawn by six bays and attended by grooms on each side. Few people were sure who was in these carriages, but they deserved a cheer anyway. Lizzie stood on tiptoe to stretch herself as closely as possible to the parade. "Which one is the Queen in?" Nobody answered. She counted the coaches as they passed, wondering who she was looking at. Next came more mounted soldiers, another band and a long line of more marching soldiers. And then the Queen. She knew it was the Queen. The carriage was magnificent. Eight pale-coloured horses this time and the carriage looked like a crown on wheels. Glittering gold in the sunshine with painted panels. A lady looked out of the window and acknowledged the crowd. Was it the Queen? It could have been. Lizzie would treasure this day for ever. The procession concluded with another company of soldiers and continued down Whitehall to the abbey.

Some in the crowd began to shuffle and move off. Lizzie just wanted to stay until she could no longer see the procession. The whole event had lasted little more than thirty minutes.

"Are we going home now?" William asked. It had been enjoyable to see all the soldiers but he did wonder what the all the fuss was about.

"Well, I tought we could go to the fair. Make a proper day of it," replied Spencer. "And if we're lucky and stay late enough, we might see some of the 'luminations."

And so, with a promise of gingerbread and a ride in the swing-boats, the family set off, accompanied by thousands of others with a like-mind, to Hyde Park.

Much of the afternoon was spent wandering through the numerous stalls and booths set up in the park. William would have liked to visit the 'freak shows' but Lizzie said it would be better to see the wild animals. To have enjoyed everything would have cost far more than they could afford, so the entertainments were chosen carefully, and generally the enjoyment came from listening to the bands and, as Lizzie said, "being there". At one point the cannon was fired again. A murmur went around the crowd. The Queen had been crowned. Shortly afterwards, all eyes turned to the direction of Green Park as a huge balloon and its two passengers ascended into the sky. They waved confidently to the crowd who waved back and watched in awe until they disappeared from view, obscured by trees and surrounding buildings. William, who had seen a balloon ascent before, explained to his sister how the contraption was able to work and added "The lady is flying her balloons everywhere now. I'm sure she'll have a terrible accident one day."

"Not today, I hope," Primrose replied. "It would spoil such a perfect day."

Late in the afternoon word spread that the royal party was leaving the abbey. The Taylors joined the surge of people hoping to catch another glimpse of the newly-crowned queen. Without time to secure a good vantage point they merely caught the end of the procession, and at some distance. By now everyone was beginning to feel exhausted from the exertions and excitement of the day. Spencer thought it was time to go home.

"It's going to be a while before the 'luminations'll be at their best and the fireworks don't start for hours." There were groans of disappointment but even Lizzie admitted her legs were aching. "I've got a little money left," Spencer continued. We can stay 'ere a bit longer, or we can spend it on a ride back 'ome. I've seen a man over there 'oo says 'e'll take us back in 'is wagon. 'E says 'e's spent all day bringing people from the fringes to the city – now 'e'll make some more money taking 'em 'ome again."

Reluctantly they agreed a ride home was very inviting, and as they rode wearily back to Stoke Newington they were entertained by spotting the coloured lamp decorations that were beginning to make their evening show.

******

Robert's day had been very different. He had no enthusiasm at all for the "artificial excitement, whipped up by the newspapers and those intending to profit from the day". It was bad enough that he had had to be part of the team who came up with the ideas for, and arranged the making of, the decorations so prominently on display outside the company's premises. They had used gas lamps and contrived every possible patriotic symbol with a crown, VR, and the rose, thistle and shamrock emblems of the countries of the United Kingdom.

He spent the morning working on some plans to try to reduce the size of an engine without decreasing its output. As he walked to the offices he was amused and irritated to see the crowds spilling out of Tooley Street station with the arrival of each train. Each wave of passengers intent on reaching the other side of the river to secure the best position for a view of the spectacle.

Robert had received a letter from his sister, Sarah, a few weeks earlier. She was intensely interested in the young Queen and had compared her own hardships and struggles in their early days in the Huron Tract to what she imagined lay ahead of for their new monarch.

> *Darlington,*
> *Ontario*
> *12th October 1837*
>
> *My Dearest Robert,*
> *I was so pleased to receive your latest letter with all your news. I do so hope your new venture will be successful.*
> *We have received the news of the succession*

to the late king and I am intrigued to hear about our new queen. She is so very young and can scarcely know anything of the world or politics. Her embarkation on her new role must be as daunting as our own on the *Charlotte*. We were sailing to the unknown, as she is entering an unknown world.

I know you will say she will not have to worry about finding food or shelter or clothing, as we had to in the early days, and she will not have to endure the cold and harsh winters we have had to adapt to. You are correct, of course, she lives a life of privilege but she will have to watch out for silver-tongued advisers who want nothing more than their own advancement, just as we had to before we understood the new ways. And she will have to overcome the disadvantage of being a woman. She will need a strong will and heart to persevere — just as we have needed the same....

He was so affected by her words that he promised his sister he would write to her with an account of the day. His intention was to read about it in the newspaper, which he was sure would cover the spectacle in minute detail. However, he thought he had better see what was happening for himself, especially as he was so close to the event. A little while after noon he left the offices and made his own way over Westminster Bridge and past the new parliament buildings being constructed after the great fire four years earlier. Everywhere he looked he could see flags, banners and garlands, decorations shaped or painted like olive branches, crowns and the royal coat of arms. Some were fashioned out of plain or coloured oil or gas lamps, waiting for dusk to show their full glory. For every one of these more ambitious ornaments there was a "VR" of every size and colour imaginable. He thought every house or property that he passed had some decoration or other. He was pleased that he had timed his excursion so that the crowds had dispersed a little, until they would return when they were alerted to the entourage leaving the abbey and another parade. He avoided the crowds but noted the clamour in the parks and the temporarily abandoned platforms lining the streets. He heard the cannon announcing the crowning of the queen and watched the balloon appear from the centre of Green Park.

His route took him along Piccadilly. Apsley House was transformed into a viewing gallery for, he guessed over a hundred people. All the mansions were littered with decorations and flowers, but most interestingly (and something he must tell Spencer about) were the orangeries that had been imported into the grounds of Devonshire House, complete with trees covered in fruit. It got his vote for the most extravagant embellishment and depressed him further about the contrasts in fortunes of people living such a short distance apart.

"You'll 'ave 'eard of the dreadful 'appenin's in Wales, I s'pose."

"Yes, I've read the reports in the newspapers. It's difficult to know the truth."

"The truth is that we wus betrayed. Soldiers already there, lyin' in wait. 'Ow'd they know if there weren't a rat?"

"We?"

"Well, y'know, Chartists."

"You're a Chartist?"

"Well, sort of. Not a member of the Society, but I signed the Petition. Did you? Waste o' time that were."

"No, I didn't. One time I might have done." Robert's thoughts went back to 1819. A day that would never leave his memory. "As you say, no point, it was never going to succeed." He began to tell Spencer about the August day that had begun with such hope and had ended in horrific tragedy. "Twenty years have passed and what progress have we made? I fear there are many wrongs to be addressed and every man has his own reasons for reform but they may differ from the issues of his neighbour. If we tackle them separately, we have no strength of numbers; the labourers in Kent don't have the same concerns as miners in Durham, miners in Durham don't have the same concerns as the silversmiths in Birmingham. But they all live in poverty, are slaves to their employers and have no means to improve their lot. The Government is constantly worried that we'll have a revolution like the French, so they have their informers and easily contain sporadic 'riots' as they like to call them. Decry the leaders, even make false allegations and dispense harsh punishments to discourage others."

"Isn't that the point of the Chartist organisation? T' 'ave a national plan?"

"You're right but if we try to tackle all the issues at once, we become a raggle-taggle mob without a common cause. The petition was clear, but it asked too much. How can you expect to get a majority vote, of the ruling class, with so many demands? If it had been kept to one or two points, it may have stood a better chance."

"Well, I'm not giving up. I want my children to 'ave a better life than we've 'ad, an' if William can vote in an election one day, it'll 'ave bin wurf it." Spencer thought it best to change the subject. "Tell me again 'ow this new invention works. I know 'ow an Archimedes screw works, we use one to raise water from the river, but 'ow can it make a ship move?"

Robert thought for a second. "Well, your screw stays still and the water moves along it, correct?"

"Yeh, that's right."

"Now imagine the water staying still and the screw being able to move."

Spencer looked blank. Robert used his hands to demonstrate. He pointed to the imaginary water with his right hand. "Look, here's this bit of water sitting on the screw, you turn the screw," he rotated his left hand in a vertical circle, "and the water moves this way."

"Mmm"

"Now, imagine the water stays here, what happens to the screw?"

"It looks like it's movin' that way!"

"Yes! And if your screw isn't fixed to a river bank but is on something floating in the river, like a boat, the water stays where it is and the screw moves the boat along."

"An' it works?"

"Oh, yes, it works very well. And there are other benefits too." Robert was full of enthusiasm for the new invention. "It disturbs the water far less than paddle wheels, so in confined spaces, like on the river, it upsets far fewer boatmen in other craft. And on the open sea it's not so affected by pitching and rolling, because it is central and under the water – so you never have one wheel submerged and the other out of the water. And… and it can be much smaller than a paddle wheel – about a tenth of the size. And…"

"Yeh, I think I've twigged." Spencer interrupted.

"She was an elegant sight. Eerie too. Three masts but no sails and moving serenely down the river. I hear she made good speed. And aptly named … *Archimedes*. I think screw-propulsion may be the choice in the future. We'll need to adapt our engines…" Robert's thoughts turned to linkages and cogs.

"Is that your work now?" Spencer enquired, hoping not to receive another lecture.

"No, we've been busy with locomotives. How I detest them! But they're everywhere now. I even have to travel by train to Greenwich when we've got work with the Admiralty. I'll never understand why they succeeded and steam-carriages didn't."

******

"I think I am going to stop reading the newspapers. They seem to wish to do nothing more than appeal to the worst side of man's nature. With a head-line of 'Horrific Accident' or 'Dreadful Disaster' we are drawn like moths to the flame to devour all the gory details. Why is that? The stories serve no purpose other than to gratify some strange thirst within us. We feel sorry for the people or their families for a fleeting moment, but we forget their names in an instant, while we can recall the details of the event for days to come – until we forget about it completely. And do we really need to know that Lord Bigacres has sold his prize racehorse, or the Countess of Moneyshire has a hat made from the feathers of eighteen ostriches, or the offspring of the Earl of Wotnot is to be married, and the peasants on the estate are so overjoyed that they have saved money they can ill-afford to buy the happy couple a silver teaspoon!"

"You don't seem y'self Robert, has sumfing 'appened?"

"No, no, not really." Robert sighed and looked up at Spencer. "I read of the death sentences for the Newport so-called traitors. Made me sick to the stomach. How can we call ourselves a civilized nation and yet pronounce such a barbaric punishment? A small paragraph beneath the article echoes my thoughts, and then the next describes the terrible dismembering of a poor railway worker who had the misfortune to fall beneath a train. You see? We are fascinated by death and gore. And what of the trial? Treason seems a harsh indictment. Foolish? Angry? Misguided? Yes, I'll accept all of those, and to be armed was extremely unwise – but not traitorous. They have no argument with the Queen; they want to improve the system, not destroy it. But as I've said many times – one law for the rich and powerful and one law... You remember Mrs Cross and her, er, enterprise?"

"Course."

"Went to prison, didn't she? Probably still there. But what of Lord Thingamy? Scoured the papers for months after you told me about it – not a word. Read about another young nob caught stealing a gold watch from a jeweller. When he first came before the court the judge announced his (Robert adopted an upper-class accent) 'disappointment at seeing a young man from such a well-regarded family in court'. Waited for weeks for the case to be tried. Nothing. And yet, some poor bloke, whose family is starving, gets caught stealing a loaf of bread. Verdict? Two months hard labour!"

Spencer sensed there was more to Robert's mood than anger with newspapers and the shallowness of people who lapped up the sensational stories but thought little of the plight of his fellow man. He didn't know what to say. He brought Robert up-to-date with news of the family and then to lighten the mood thought he would repeat a funny story told to Lizzie and the other 'below stairs' staff by Mr Johnston, the butler at the 'Big House'.

"They was 'avin' a big do. Primrose 'ad 'ad to 'elp prepare all kinds of stuff. Ice cream was the 'ardest. Anyway the meal was over an' the ladies 'ad gone and the port was flowin'. One of the guests starts talking baht 'is bruvver in Jamaicay and 'ow it's takin' an unreasonable time to get the compensation for loosin' all 'is slaves. Well! This other cove – Johnston says 'e's something to do wiv Wilberforce, y' know the anti-slave man, some relative or uvver – anyway he slams 'is glass on the table and goes on abaht 'ow it should be the slaves that's compensated for their mis-treatment an' everyfing. Johnston says 'e's never 'eard such a to-do. Fought they was going to 'ave a duel or somefing. 'Parently they 'ad to be kept apart by the others."

Robert smiled but it didn't make him feel any better. He thought of Louise and if he had made the right decision to leave her behind. Was she right that they couldn't have had a future together? He had often thought of seeing her again, but she was so determined. "Sometimes I think about joining my sister in Canada. But she says she frequently regrets the move. Says they were 'seduced by the honeyed words of the Land Agents'. Says the place is full of pensioned-off soldiers. Oh, there's the rich there too – carrying on with their own little bit of England. Some of them have been given positions that make them think they *are* someone, but put them out in the backwoods (that's what they call the forests) and they'd be starved dead in weeks. I had a letter from Sarah yesterday. It was written before the worst of the winter – I wonder how it has been."

Robert and Arthur were working late in the engine shed. The engine had to be ready for trials the next day, and a seemingly innocuous alteration to a gasket had caused a major problem that needed to be rectified.

"We could try this," Arthur showed Robert where he meant to redirect a pipe to connect in a different place.

"It could work," Robert agreed, and the men set about the task.

"You know what tonight is?" Arthur could never work without holding a conversation on some completely random subject that popped in to his head.

"What's that?" Robert replied as he struggled to fit a spanner in an inaccessible part of the engine.

"Census night."

"Oh, yes, I'd forgotten. Mrs P was asking when my birthday is yesterday. I thought she was going to give me a birthday present at first, but then she asked where I was born too, and I realised... There – that's got it," Robert broke off the conversation as the nut finally budged.

"Well, that's the thing. I was wondering. Should you be on the record at your lodgings, or here? After all, this is where you're spending the night."

"Yes, but this is a place of work, not a dwelling."

"I suppose you're right. I can't see why they need to know so much about us though. Have you seen the form? Feels like we're being spied on. What with that and the registrations for everything. Government'll know all about us soon. Nowhere to hide!" he added this in a threatening tone of voice.

"Do you want to hide?"

"Well, no, but why do they need it all? How many people live in England? Must be millions. Who's ever going to have time to look at all the information? And why do they need to know so much? Can't imagine anyone would ever be interested to know that Sarah Jones is a dressmaker, or Thomas Smith is a bricklayer."

"Not just England, whole of Great Britain. There's always been censuses – just this one's a bit more detailed. Used to be so they knew who to conscript into the army, I think. But now it's probably more about taxes. Can't see it'll be very accurate though."

"Looks like that'll work. Just got to connect these two…" Arthur carried on working as they talked. "What do you mean?"

"Well, every house has a form to fill in, right?"

"Yes."

"And suppose you can't read?"

"Ah, I guess the enumerator will help then."

"And suppose your landlord doesn't know much about you, and, unlike Mrs P, hasn't bothered to find out? They'll just make something up."

"Mmm."

"And what about vagrants and gypsies? How they going to count all of them?"

"Well…"

"And can you imagine some clerk in his shiny leather boots and smart coat and trousers going to Whitechapel or somesuch? The rats… and the smell… and twenty houses to a court, four or five rooms to a house? That's, what, a hundred to record – I don't think he'll want to stay long – even if the 'householder' knows anything about the poor wretches that live there. No, can't see it working."

Eventually their work was done. The sun was just rising as they packed the tools away.

"Hardly worth going home, is it? We'll have to be back here in a few hours."

Robert shrugged, "What else can we do?"

"Follow me." Arthur took Robert to a room on the top floor. It was empty except for an old wooden bench seat, a cupboard and a table. Arthur went to the cupboard and took out a couple of blankets.

"Yours, I presume," Robert said. "You've done this before!"

Arthur handed him a blanket and grinned. "Bench, table or floor?"

Robert chose the floor, as it looked the least uncomfortable. He spread the blanket beneath him and scrunched his coat into a makeshift pillow. Sleep did not follow quickly.

"Have you ever been to the Gardens?" Arthur asked just as Robert felt he had been dozing off.

"What gardens? Oh, you mean Vauxhall?"

"Yes."

"No." He turned onto his side, away from Arthur who was stretched out on the bench.

"We're going, Alfred and I, when the season starts, with Harriet and Mary from next-door. You know, the beauties I told you about. You could come with us. I'm sure they could find a friend to bring, so you wouldn't be a wallflower."

Robert hesitated. "It's a bit, er, rough around the edges now isn't it. I mean, it's not as …" he couldn't think of the right word.

"Oh, you going all high and mighty now, are you?" Arthur teased. "No, it's not what it was, must admit, but it's still a grand evening. Go on. Say you'll come. And you know, it still …"

"… *only costs a shillin'*" they chorused, laughing.

******

Robert was not enthusiastic about the forthcoming evening out, but he dressed smartly. He knew the evening was going to be expensive so he walked to the gates where they had arranged to meet, making sure he got there in plenty of time and before the others arrived in a hackney carriage. Harriet and Mary locked arms with Arthur and

Alfred and inspected Robert as he was introduced to their friend, Alice.

Alice, like the rest of the group, was about ten years younger than Robert. She had long straw-coloured hair that she plaited and twisted around her head, making her round face look even rounder. Her dress was simply cut, with long sleeves and made from a creamy cotton fabric printed with small blue flowers. She carried a plain cream shawl over one arm, ready for when the evening turned chilly. Robert guessed that she had made her outfit herself as, hanging from her wrist was a reticule, made of the same material as her dress.

After a reserved bobbing and bowing, she too, took Robert's arm, to be escorted into the gardens. The men duly paid their two shillings (one for themselves and one for their companion) at the entrance booth and entered the gardens. Alfred thought they should book a dinner booth, which the ladies enthusiastically endorsed, and so that was arranged too.

Harriet and Mary wanted to visit the dioramas but Alice said she should like to wander around the walks and gardens as it was still light and the evening was warm. While Arthur and his party diverted to the dioramas, Alice and Robert strolled leisurely around the gardens. Feeling awkward at the silence, Robert asked the least intrusive question he could think of.

"Have you always lived in Lambeth?"

"Oh no, I was born and lived in Kent. My pa was a fisherman, and his father, and his father before that. Flounders, dabs, rig. Cod and haddock sometimes." she fell silent, recollecting those days that seemed so long ago now.

"When did you come here, then?"

"Oh, about fifteen years past." Her voice broke a little and Robert sensed it was difficult for her to speak of it. She composed herself and continued. "There was a bad storm and my father and two brothers were lost." She paused. "My mother said she couldn't bear to see the sea again after that and moved west to find work. Ended up near here with me and my two sisters."

Robert wished he hadn't broached the subject and told her about his early life in Westmorland, describing the fells and the sheep farming.

"There's not much in the way of mountains round here, is there? You must miss that."

"Sometimes I miss the wild mountain air. It's all so flat here, and the horizon is always full of buildings."

They continued talking, Robert explaining briefly how he came to be in London, and Alice telling him about her job as a maid-of-all-work in the same house where Harriet and Mary were employed. As they walked, they passed bands and orchestras, caught the uncertain high notes of a soprano attempting an operatic aria, noted jugglers and other 'street' entertainers, each drawing a small crowd. There was a theatrical show about to start in the Rotunda, but Alice said she was happier just to wander and see the sights. They continued talking when suddenly there was a blast from a whistle. Alice started and Robert turned abruptly to see where the noise had come from. The couple collided and Alice hand came to rest on Robert's lapel, to steady herself. At that moment two more whistle blasts sounded and the trees suddenly filled with thousands of coloured lamps, giving the whole area a magical feel. Their eyes locked for an instant before Robert offered profuse apologies for the collision and hoped she was not hurt.

"No, no, not at all. Perhaps we should return to the Grove and find the others."

They made their way through the crowds to find their allotted supper booth. The other couples were already there and had obviously already consumed a few rum punches.

"Ah, there you are!" Alfred said, moving closer to Mary to make room for the late-comers. Arthur signalled to a waiter and supper was ordered.

Robert had expected a more substantial meal, given the cost of it, and wished he had eaten some bread and cheese before leaving home, as alcohol and an empty stomach were not a good mix for him. He had heard the story of the Vauxhall carver who could cover the whole Gardens with the meat from a single ham. He began to wonder if it were true. The waiters were very attentive and produced more punch and port almost before the party had thought to order it. Alice insisted on plain lemonade as she had to be at work early the next day. Robert, partly to keep her company, but mostly because he thought it was a good idea, spent the rest of the evening drinking lemonade too.

As supper-time progressed, any façade of gentility amongst the clientele declined. Arthur,

Alfred and their partners, like the revellers around them, drank liberally and grew noisier. They fell into singing songs and were much amused by:

> "WAITER, waiter! a plate of ham!"
> Cried a Cit, in a tone of grimace;
> When the wind, which gave the door a slam,
> Blew the slice in the Briton's face.
>
> The wafery bit stuck to him like glue,
> When he bawled, with a terrible "damn!"
> "I do not swear I can see through you,
> But I can through your slice of ham!

Alice whispered to Robert that she should like to see something of the fireworks and so Robert hoped he had made Arthur understand that they would meet them at the entrance gate when the Gardens closed. They made their way to the grounds set aside for the display. They had both seen the rockets, in previous seasons, making their way up into the sky, but were intrigued to see what other displays would be available to the audience inside. Robert paid the entrance fee and they chose a vantage point. Alice 'ooh'ed and 'aah'ed along with the crowd and jumped and laughed at every unexpected bang. Robert marvelled at some of the colours and effects, and at the height some of the rockets achieved, but in all honesty, he was a little disappointed in the show.

When the fireworks ended, they shuffled along with the rest of the throng to the entrance gate. Robert wished he had arranged to meet ten minutes earlier and avoid the rush. They linked arms so that they wouldn't get separated with the jostling of the crowd. Robert held one hand over his wallet, for fear of being pick-pocketed and warned Alice to keep her bag tightly grasped in her hand. By the time Arthur and the others joined them most of the crowd had dispersed, and most of the carriages who had waited strategically for fares had also disappeared. Luckily, one who was used to collecting the stragglers returned and the six friends clambered aboard.

Robert had been concerned that the small carriage would be a squash for all six of them, but he needn't have worried as Harriet sat gracefully on Arthur's lap, and Mary, less gracefully, on Alfred's. Robert and Alice sat side-by-side, gazing wearily at their friends, and being less drunk than they were, not enjoying their raucous mood. Alice's house was the first on the journey and on arriving, Robert gallantly alighted first to give Alice his hand and help her off the carriage. Despite her tiredness, she was in no hurry to let go of his hand and kept hers resting lightly on his as they wished each other goodnight. Having re-boarded, Robert gave the coachman the signal to continue to his own home. On arriving, Robert gave Arthur a note to pay his part of the fare when they reached their destination. He was dismayed to find he had emptied his wallet completely.

"Never mind," he thought, "It *had* been a grand evening."

21

1844

Robert and Spencer were enjoying a rare day's fishing. At least, their rods were resting, supported by sticks and angled above the water, and their lines were in the river. Robert was sitting up gazing across the water and watching the Sunday afternoon crowd out for their stroll. Spencer lay on the river bank with his jacket rolled up to make a pillow and the warmth of the sun penetrating his shirt sleeves. Two birds flew overhead, soaring effortlessly in the air-currents.

"Do yer fink *we'll* ever fly?" Spencer said sleepily. Robert turned towards him.

"What, you mean in one of Mr Green's balloons?"

"No, he's at the mercy of the winds. No, I mean like birds – free to go wherever we want."

Robert thought for a minute.

"I think we'd need a balloon of some kind. We'd never be able to do it by attaching wings to our arms – not strong enough."

"Wouldn't you like to be up there? Looking down on everyfing goin' on below. An' fink 'ow quick the birds can get abaht cos they don't 'ave to stick to the roads."

"Yes, but how could you direct the balloon?"

"One of yer propeller fings – would they work?"

"Shouldn't think so, anyway you'd need an engine up there to drive it – the weight would be so much the balloon would have to be huge!" His mind wandered to wondering just *how* big it would need to be but not knowing enough about the lifting capabilities of coal gas or any other gas, he gave up.

"How's young Primrose and William getting on?"

"William's doin' well for hisself. If I don' watch out, 'e'll be after *my* job! Got a real talent wiv plants, 'e 'as. An' Primmy's doin' well too. She don't like the sewing, like 'er muvver but she ain't just a kitchen maid, no more – got a proper position wiv the cook. But never mind all that. 'Ow's that young lady of yours?"

"Oh, still with her sister," he replied without elaborating.

Following their evening at Vauxhall, Robert had pestered Arthur for Alice's place of work and wanted to know her working hours. He then set about wandering in the correct vicinity at an appropriate time in the hope that their paths would 'accidently' cross. After several weeks of mis-timing he eventually spotted her walking along the pavement towards him. His heart raced as he rehearsed, for the hundredth time, what he would say.

"Good evening, Alice," he blurted out. "No, no, too formal," he thought. "A surprised 'Hallo' would have been better."

Alice smiled, genuinely pleased to see him again. she bobbed a curtsey and immediately started talking about their evening together, how much she had enjoyed it, how little she had been looking forward to it, and, when recalling the fright the whistles had given them both, reached out and touched Robert's shoulder to reinforce the shared experience. They walked towards Alice's home, talking easily together, any thoughts of pre-rehearsed speeches long dismissed. As they reached her door, Robert finally found the courage to ask if she would like to go with him one day for a picnic in Greenwich Park. She thought it was "a lovely idea" and the excursion was arranged for the following Sunday. After that they had had many meetings, picnics, suppers, visits to the Surrey Zoological Gardens, and anything the great metropolis could offer. It had been a perfect summer.

In the autumn, Robert was invited to tea with Alice's mother at Rotherhithe. She was a tall, gaunt woman, greying hair and a face that revealed nothing of what she was thinking. Even her smile was without any warmth. At first sight, Robert had not taken to her but the afternoon passed pleasantly, and she offered no objection to the couple continuing to meet.

The following spring, Robert was set to propose to Alice, when fate took over. Alice's mother had 'a turn' at her workplace, she was sent home and Alice was sent for. (Alice's other two sisters were in service; Emily in Warwickshire and Caroline in Dorset, so being the nearest and eldest, the message was sent to Alice.)

"Probably no more than a fainting fit," explained the doctor, who had made daily visits since the event.

Alice had never seen her mother looking so ill. She felt there was more to her mother's illness than just tight corsets and insufficient food but was certain the doctor was going to do nothing more. She promised to stay and nurse her mother until her health improved.

"Thank you, doctor," she said firmly. "I think we can manage without you now."

The doctor prescribed a 'tonic', took his fee and left.

After few weeks of attentive nursing, and rebuilding her strength, first with beef tea and then with more substantial meals and occasional walks outside, Alice's mother began to regain her independent disposition and insisted on both of them returning to work.

Unfortunately, in the August, the mother had another 'turn'. This time it was more serious.

"You must go to your mother," Alice's employer insisted. "We can make do. Mary and Harriet are good girls. Do not worry," he continued when he saw the concern on Alice's face, "You

191

have worked here for many years. The position will be here when you are ready to return."

******

"Convulsion," the doctor announced pompously. "We find it quite common amongst the women at the works. *Female hysteria*, is the medical term."

Feeling the doctor had no more to offer her mother, Alice paid him and said he need not return.

Alice set about rebuilding her mother's strength again, but this time she did not respond so well. She frequently complained of intense, blinding, brain-splitting headaches and suffered several more fits, each getting more severe and long-lasting. Her mood fell deeper into despondency and her speech became incoherent. By September her body could take no more and she passed away after a last, devastating convulsion.

Alice was completely overcome with despair. She had had to watch her mother suffer terrible agonies and felt helpless and inadequate. She was angry that her mother had to die that way. She was angry that the White Lead Manufactory regarded suffering and death as an acceptable consequence of working there. She was angry that she'd had to deal with everything on her own. She was angry that the sea had stolen her father and brothers. She was angry, and inconsolable.

As much as Robert wanted to ease her pain, he knew that it was not the right time to suggest a marriage. She needed to come to terms with the events of the year and to find her spirit again. So, when her sister Caroline suggested she went to live with her in Dorset for a while, Robert encouraged her to make the journey.

It was a frustration to Robert that, although he made frequent visits to Portsmouth and Dover on testing trials and other engineering matters, he never managed to reach Weymouth or anywhere in close quarters to Alice. He had written to her constantly, and he was overjoyed, when in the Spring of '43 she had replied. He always kept her latest letter in his breast-pocket and took the most recent out to read a passage to Spencer:

.... We have had the most wonderful weather here this week. Caroline and I went for a glorious walk along the cliff top. The air was so still that the heat seemed to come up from the ground as much as it fell from the sun.

The sheep and cattle on the hillsides had to find shelter by the scrubby trees and hedges wherever they could.

Although we have walked that way many times, the sight of the bay below us as we reach the crown of the hill, always lifts my spirits. It is so perfectly formed, sheltering the fishing boats from the wilder ocean.

Mother could not bear to see the sea, but I shall never tire of this place. I do hope, darling Robert, that you will be able to see it one day too....

"I think she is getting back to her old self," Robert said cheerfully. "I still live in hope."

22

1845

"Houghton, you will have to do this. Lambert's in Birmingham, and Thomson is delayed in Dover." Mr Field spoke with gravity as he gave Robert an assignment. "These plans have to be in Greenwich tomorrow. I cannot emphasise enough how important they are, and that they must only be seen by the people at the Admiralty. Come in early tomorrow and collect them from the safe. Then take them straight to Greenwich."

The next morning, Robert boarded the train and sat in his favoured seat, next to the window and back to the engine. The plans were rolled in a cylindrical leather case marked with the Government broad-arrow, which he held securely across his knees. It was vital to keep the plans safe, and secret: there was information about engines and propellers that the Admiralty would not want getting into the wrong hands! The train was busy and his carriage was filling with passengers before its departure. To make more room he propped the tube on the seat between himself and the window. No-one would be able to steal it from him that way. His manoeuvring seemed to annoy the gentleman sitting next to him. "There's no pleasing some people," Robert thought to himself, "I only moved to give him more room."

The engine gave a whistle and slowly pulled out of the terminus. His neighbour took this as a signal to take a very elegant snuff box from his inside pocket. With the snuff in his fingers, he inhaled deeply and then sneezed, very ostentatiously Robert thought, into a handkerchief which he extracted from another pocket just in time. Two ladies sitting opposite them began to talk, without any thought of keeping their conversation from being overheard.

"I do wish we could reserve a private compartment. It is so much more pleasant to travel by carriage than on this contraption, is it not?"

The second lady nodded in agreement "Oh yes, you just never know who you will have to share with on these *trains*." She enunciated the word with a certain disgust, as if she were making the journey on the night-cart.

Robert thought that if Mr Dickens were on board, the present company would become characters in his next novel. "What would he call them?" Robert wondered. "Mr Broad... Mr Oliver Broadman and the Misses Agnes and Ethel Littlemind." he smiled to himself and reached into his pocket to take out the latest edition of *Jerrold's Magazine*.

They had not been travelling long before the train stopped again at a station. More passengers came aboard and settled in their seats. Disturbed from his reading, Robert gazed out of the window. The railway line was remarkable, elevated above the hustle of the streets on its long line of arches. But more railways were encroaching into the city, from the east and from the west and the north. Whole streets had been knocked down to make way for them. The landlords had received compensation, but Robert sympathised with the tenants who were evicted from their homes with no arrangements for finding a new one. The bustle of the city gave way to fields, and dozens of ships could be seen on the river. He watched for a while but then they were held at a signal and so he returned to his story.

It was only when the train jerked to a halt that he realised he had reached his destination already.

He was concerned that the delay by the signal would make him late for his appointment. He rushed up, opened the carriage door and hurried to the station exit. Just as he was about to leave the railway premises he realised that the leather tube, that should have been slung over his shoulder, was not there. A dreadful panic spread over him. If he were to lose those plans … it didn't bear thinking about. He'd lose his job for sure, and probably worse. Luckily the train was at its terminus, so wasn't about to move off again soon. He turned and rushed back towards the carriage he had just left, colliding with the unhappy ladies from earlier. He apologised profusely and continued to the carriage. Coming towards him was the gentleman from the carriage, bearing the tube thrust out in front of him.

"I believe this is yours, sir!" he announced in a deep resonant voice.

"Oh, yes, thank you, so much." Relief melted the panic, and then the gentleman introduced himself.

"I am Captain Birch. I believe we may have an appointment."

Despite the day's inauspicious start, the meeting went well. Apart from Robert with the technical knowledge of engines and so on, there were several navy personnel and a representative from the propeller company. Commodore Parker was leading the discussions. He had been a midshipman at Trafalgar and had served in many ships since then.

"I am aware the propeller is proving advantageous over paddle wheels." The assembled company sensed a 'but' was to follow. "But can you not see the disadvantages? Steam power requires engines and engines require coal. And both of these require space! Space below deck is limited. Fitting engines will reduce space for supplies and provisions which in turn reduces the duration of the expedition. Using sail alone is a far better option."

"This is true, sir," Captain Birch agreed, "But you must recall the great danger to the ships and the men when *Erebus* was trapped in the ice on her recent expedition with *Terror* to Antarctica. If it had not been for good luck, both ships may have been lost, or at least severely damaged. And we are not intending the propulsion of the ships to be by propeller alone. No, sir, sail will still be the preferred method. When *Erebus* and *Terror* sail on their voyage of discovery to the Arctic, they will be as well prepared as science allows. We don't want any unforeseen mishaps this time!"

"The propellers are purely for auxiliary power, as the Captain says, to aid the ships if becalmed or caught in ice," Robert said to reinforce Birch's argument. "The intention is to use adapted locomotive engines. Imagine a locomotive with its wheels removed – it becomes a much smaller structure than a conventional paddle wheel engine, and of course requires less fuel."

"Nor will the ships have to carry coal to furnish the whole journey," another added, "just enough to cover these 'emergencies'. And because they are not going to be in constant use, the propeller will be stored onboard the ship – to reduce drag – and only deployed when needed."

"Good Heavens!" exclaimed Commodore Parker, "Then explain to me how this can be done, and how you can cut a hole in the hull of ship and not expect the sea to sink it."

Robert showed the commodore the drawings, explained where the engine would be sited and how the mechanism for raising the propeller in and out of the water would work. Finally, it was agreed. They would try new designs for the ships' propellers and install the engines to drive the propellers. A provisional sailing date for the expedition was set for the beginning of May and a demonstration would be held in due course to show the practicality of raising the 'screw' in and out of the stern of the ships.

Robert and Captain Birch returned to 'town' on the same train. The Captain entertained Robert for the whole journey with tales of his polar expeditions to the Antarctic. Robert could barely conceive of travelling all that way from the shores of England, let alone exploring a land with such a hostile climate. He was pleased to be involved with the plans for the latest venture to the 'Far North' but happy to let the sailors make the journey, and leave him behind.

As winter turned to spring, Robert made frequent visits to Woolwich to oversee and track the progress of fitting the engines in expeditionary ships. At the end of April all the interested parties, including the two captains appointed for the voyage, engineers, shipwrights, and a small delegation of commodores and admirals visited Woolwich to see the progress on the ships for themselves. They saw how the hulls were strengthened to cope with the pressure of ice, the method of stowing the propeller on the deck was explained to them and they inspected the partly installed engines that would be used.

23

May 1845

Robert kissed Alice gently on the cheek. "Love," he said quietly. She was busy stirring supper in a pot on the range. He pulled a chair to face her and sat on it, resting one arm on the table. Before she could turn and tell him her news, he shuffled and started to speak.

"I've got something to tell you," he began. He stared steadfastly at his hands, as if concentrating on rolling them together would ease the effect of what he was about to say. "I have to go north with a Naval ship."

"Don't worry, love," Alice soothed, "You've been away before on your trials. Where are you going? Scotland?"

"No, much further. Almost to the North Pole. This isn't going to be weeks or months. It'll be years. Two, three, maybe five if we succeed in finding the route."

Alice stopped stirring and knelt in front of him. She wanted to yell her questions at him, but instead unsteadily asked, "Why so long?"

"Another exploration. Past Scotland and Greenland. The plan is to go north of Canada and find a route to the Pacific Ocean. A trade route that way will save so much time. Not having to go around the Cape of Good Hope."

Alice wasn't concerned about trade routes. "But why you? You're not even in the Navy!"

"Not yet, but I will be."

"What?"

"I've tried to refuse. But they are insisting. Arthur has to go too. Apparently, the people we've been dealing with have been impressed with our work and of course it's kudos for the company to have two of its engineers on such a voyage. We're going to be made naval personnel, with a rank and title 'Chief Engineer'. The pay will be good and you'll get an allotment while I'm away."

Alice was only half-listening. The thought of Robert being away for *years* was uppermost in her mind. She couldn't believe it. How would she cope? They talked long into the evening. The enormity of the venture was overwhelming. Alice's news would have to wait.

Robert drew a rough map, explaining the planned voyage. He exaggerated the size of Great

Britain, making the distances seem a little less formidable than he knew them to be. Aware that Alice would be alone in London while he was gone, he suggested that she returned to Dorset to be near Caroline.

"You can go as soon as we can arrange everything. The ships will be sailing very soon. The men fitting the ships have been working thirteen-hour shifts. They even have to take their meals on site. I can move to lodgings at the dockyard and be on hand when queries arise. We can both leave Lambeth. When I return, we can decide where to set up a new home."

The next few days were busy and hectic. They settled on renting a cottage in Weymouth and Robert arranged for Alice to collect her allotment of thirteen pounds per month, on which she could live comfortably until his return. Alice packed a trunk with some essential possessions to take with her on the train and carriage journey to Dorset.

A horse-omnibus took them the few miles to the Nine Elms terminus. They barely spoke, neither knowing what to say. Parting was difficult for them both, and Alice had still not told Robert the 'news' she had been so eager to relate just a week or so earlier. She had decided that it was better that he did not know as she thought he would worry while he was away – and he had enough to cope with. Her plan was to get the news to him as soon as she knew he was returning. Then meeting their child would not be such a great shock.

******

Robert retuned home and made the arrangements for the last of their belongings to be taken by cart to the cottage. He wrote two long letters, one to Spencer and Lizzie and the other to Sarah, explaining where he was going and why he would not be in touch for a while. He considered for some time whether or not to write to Louise. He decided against it: she may not still be at the same address, and more significantly, they had deliberately not kept in touch. She had insisted their lives would go in different directions. He loved Alice, he was sure of that, but it was different to what he had shared with Louise. He knew he could never recapture those days and it was right to leave them as happy memories.

He then left for Woolwich and a new life as a Chief Engineer in the Royal Navy. He met with

Arthur, who had been assigned the same post on board *HMS Terror*. Their familiarity with the railway locomotive engines had secured their positions. The irony of it being his hated form of transport was not lost on Robert.

A few days later, with a full crew, the ships left the dockyard at Woolwich for an initial journey to Greenhithe. They did not deploy their sails but were towed by two paddle steamers. A short way down the Thames, Robert was surprised to see the crew of *Terror* dispensing with their tow.

"Captain Crozier must have given orders to use the engine," he remarked to another of *Erebus*'s crew who was standing alongside him on deck.

Final arrangements and adjustments were made to the ships, and on Saturday the seventeenth of May, their voyage of discovery began.

Whale Fish Island,
Greenland
8th July 1845

My darling Alice,

   As you see I am fit and well, apart from being heartsick for not seeing you and being with you. Our journey so far has been uneventful, even a little tedious, although there was some excitement when we spotted a pod of whales a few days ago. We have tested the propellers and all is well. I have kept myself occupied by keeping a journal of the voyage and making sketches of the ships and crew. Many of the men are from the north, like me, and from Scotland. I expect the Navy thinks we can cope better with the cold weather! We also have a library on board, so there is no shortage of reading matter.

   At the beginning I was _very_ seasick. This was not helped by a severe storm a few days after we embarked. All the ships in our little convoy had to take shelter just off the Suffolk coast. No harm was done and now I have properly got my 'sea-legs'. I think if I were to stand on solid ground, I should probably fall over!

I have had to learn how to address the members of our company and who is my 'equal', or 'superior', and who belongs to the 'lower ranks'. The commissioned officers have quite luxurious quarters and the seamen swing in hammocks. I share a cabin with the other two Warrant Officers, Misters Terry and Weekes, the Boatswain and Carpenter.

At the beginning of July we bade farewell to the ships who had towed us as far as the Orkneys. The officers had a farewell dinner and there was much cheering and hollering from the crews as the ships parted company.

So, do not worry about me, my darling. All is progressing very well and we shall soon be on our voyage of discovery.

Every day will take me more miles further away from you but I prefer to think that every day I am away is one day closer to being with you again.

We have sailed to Greenland with a transport ship as a companion. The crews are unloading provisions for us as I write. As well as coal for the boilers (for the propeller and the heating) we have jars and tins of food and 5 freshly killed and butchered bullocks – as well as enough rum to float the Armada!

I wish you could be with me here and see the wonderful sights; a sun that never dips below the horizon and the magical ethereal blue of the ice. I never imagined ice could be so beautiful.

I hope you are finding the cottage in Weymouth satisfactory and the air agreeable. Please send my good wishes to Caroline when you see her next.

I must close now as they are calling for all communications to be collected and transferred to the transport ship before she departs and returns to Woolwich.

I send you a thousand kisses   X X
and have marked the paper   X X X X X
where you may find them.   X X

Your ever-loving and devoted husband,

Robert

Please, my darling, when you receive this, will you send a note to Sarah and Spencer to let them know all is well?

Robert Houghton is a fictional character but two men really were recommended to the Admiralty by the company Maudslay, Son and Field for Franklin's Arctic expedition in 1845.

They were John Gregory, in his late 50s, married to Hannah, with several children including a baby son, and James Thompson, age about 30, unmarried.
They served as Chief Engineers on *HMS Erebus* and *HMS Terror*, respectively.

All of the 134 men who sailed on from Greenland lost their lives on the unsuccessful mission.

This book is dedicated to them and the families they left behind.

Acknowledgements and References

Acknowledgements and thanks to the following, whose works and facilities have enabled me to include accurate details and accounts of the events portrayed in this book:

Bude Castle Heritage Centre, Bude, Cornwall
Devon libraries online reference
History of Science Museum, Broad Street, Oxford
National Archives
National Maritime Museum, Greenwich

Various contemporary newspaper reports
Various internet sites, including:
http://www.bl.uk/onlinegallery (maps and images)
https://www.british-history.ac.uk
http://www.gracesguide.co.uk
http://www.scottishheritage.net (Scott Reekie)
https://shippingwondersoftheworld.com
https://en.wikipedia.org

Topics for further reading about the early 19th Century:

Abolition of Slavery
Canada Company
Canals
Coaching and stage coaches
Factories and working conditions
Loddiges Botanical Gardens
London Bridge
Parliament Fire of 1834
Polar exploration
Radicals and Political Reform
    Chartists
    Luddites
    Swing riots
    Tolpuddle martyrs

Rail transport
Rainhill trials
Spitalfields Acts
Steam road transport
Steam ships: (paddle steamers and propeller driven)
Theatre and entertainment
Vauxhall Gardens
The lives and work of:
    Marc and Isambard Brunel
    Goldsworthy Gurney
    Walter Hancock
    Maudslay, Sons and Field
    George Shillibeer

Printed in Great Britain
by Amazon